Tim Cooks is a gestalt entity. The contributors are:

- Amy Brown-Lyons

- Carlos Barton

- Daniel Skentelbery

- Francesca Cannon

- Katherine Emberton

- Lavinia Ioana Udrea

- Matthew J. Randall

- Suad Agar Eyer

- Zachary Winger

The project was overseen by Yvonne Skipper and Joe Reddington. The cover image was provided by Raghavan Prabhu, via a creative commons licence.

The group cheerfully acknowledges the wonderful help given by:

- Nick Garnett

- Lisa McWilliams

- Matt Coombe-Boxall

- Michael Murray

- Patrick Leman

- The Be More Team

- Keele University Library

- Blackwell's Bookshop

It's been a wonderful opportunity, and everyone involved has been filled with incredible enthusiasm.

The group started to plan out their novel at 9.15 on Monday 1st June 2015 and com-

pleted their last proof reading at 15.00 on
Friday 5th June 2015.

4

Walking Through the Ashes

Tim Cooks

5th June 2015

2

Prologue

Through the ashes, the house could barely be seen from afar. At that particular moment, it wasn't exactly what you call a welcoming cottage, but this world was not a fairytale world. Inside the house there were three people left. It doesn't seem like much, but after the events of the last few months, three people could make a place seem crowded. The first of them finds the last bottled water in the fridge and a box of cookies by the no-longer-working sink. The second woman sits at the table watching the child drawing a yellow sun on a wrinkled piece of paper with his crayons.

The child placed his sun in the middle of the piece of paper like it was the most important element in his drawing. The sun was white in the middle and then the child progressively changed his colour from yellow to red, making it look quite ominous.

"Dylan, why did you draw this sun?" asks the second woman.

"I miss seeing the Sun. I waited all winter for the summer to come but every day was too cloudy. I miss playing outside." explains the child.

"Poor Dylan, he has been through so much." Thought the second woman and smiles in response to the child, gently touching his face.

The first woman entered the dining room with a tray of drinks and the box of cookies.

Dylan, please put away your drawings so we can have something to eat!' shouts the first woman.

The child shuffles his papers to the floor and drops the pack of crayons on top of them, expectant of his box of cookies. The first woman places a glass of water and a few cookies in front of the child, and two cups of coffee for the second woman, and herself, and they open the box of cookies and they all began to eat.

"It hasn't rained in a few days, " the second woman points out.

The first woman looks at her strangely and mutters, "I wouldn't expect it to. That would be way more luck than we'd ever get."

"You're probably right, " agreed the second woman in resignation.

"I like the rain, " the boy speaks louder, "It makes it less dusty."

"Eat your food Dylan, " said the second woman quietly.

The three sat in silence, each chewing away at their sweet snacks and slowly sipping their drinks.

A light breeze can be heard dragging the dust across the windows. Something creaks outside, probably a neighbour's door coming off of its hinges. Nothing that phases these three any more.

"Thank you Lily, by the way, " the first woman blurted out, "for watching Dylan while I was away."

"Tamie, you know you would have done the same for me. He might as well be my brother too, and he needed help, " replied the second woman. "And what else did I have to do anyway, it's not like I was busy", she added bitterly.

The three finish up their snacks, and the Tamie gathered their bottles and plastic wrapping in her hands and takes them back to the kitchen. She dropped the trash into the bin under the sink and pulls the now full bag out of the bin. There were no garbage men left, so she steps out the back door with the bag in hand and hurls it as far as she could over the back fence. She could have been throwing it into the neighbour's yard, but there weren't any neighbours left.

Back in the dining room Lily and Dylan pick

his papers back up off the floor and spread them out across the table. They were all covered in dust and ashes, like everything else in the house, but somehow they were still brightly coloured and beautiful. Lily and the Dylan were admiring the pictures together when the other woman reenters the room.

The three of them sit together at the table, drawing and talking for hours. They have made a strange family, but a necessary one. Like the rest of the people in this new world, they have paved their way through disaster, and this was what they had left.

Book 1

Monday, May 31, 2032

Radio Broadcast,   12:32 p.m.

We interrupt our regular programming at the request of the United States Federal Government.

A civil authority has issued an alert - stand by.

We interrupt our programming - this is a national emergency.

This is not a test.

To participate in the emergency broadcast system in your local area. The following message has been verified. That a supervolcano under Yellowstone Nation Park has erupted.

All residents of the United States should seek out and prepare to take shelter.

Please stay tuned for further announcements.

Tamie,   12:40 p.m.

The questions were perfect, just as the lecturer had set them out in class a couple of weeks before. All the previous week's revision felt like it was coming together as I reached the end of my first question.

I was totally in the zone, oblivious to all the coughs and squeaking tables round the hall. All that was there was this exam paper and myself. My eyes were focused on the the paper, but I was already thinking about the plans I had made with my roommate for after the exam had finished. Whilst this wasn't the last exam of the finals, we'd decided that we had plenty of time between exams, so we could afford a break that evening. After a couple of drinks at the bar I suggested that we go catch the late showing of some old horror films, in a recently converted basement cinema. As my hand conducted the pen across the room my mind was anywhere other than the exam hall. At the start of the exam I had be thankful that I had not drawn the short straw and that my table would not be one of those duds that wobbles away throughout the whole exam causing myself to suffer the paranoia that all my classmates were quietly planning my death because of the annoying sound of a wobbly table. However, when my table seemed to momentarily collapse causing my rigid hand to put a line through my paper, I must admit I was fairly surprised to look around the hall and see everybody else had had the same experience. Before the invigilators could remind us that anybody actively looking at other students papers could lead to our test papers being destroyed, the university's fire alarm system started to blare.

In a loud voice the lead invigilator, an elderly man who had been kind enough to allow us the benefit of starting out exam a couple of minutes before the authorised examination time, climbed on to a chair. From his elevated position he instructed us firstly to place our pens on our desk tops, and then told us that we would have to sit tight and await further instructions. The first few minutes passed quickly as everybody looked around the room, not at each other, but rather trying just to look anywhere where another person wasn't. After those first couple of minutes the novelty of the fire alarm, a siren interspersed with a calm computerised voice asking us to leave the building, started to give me a headache. a feeling of distress gradually settled at the bottom of my stomach, whatever it was that had caused this disruption was greatly welcomed, especially as I was starting to wonder whether I would ever be able to get back into that exam mind set that I had found at the start of the exam.

Before I could give it anymore thought, the whole hall rippled as the silence that had settled under the siren was interrupted by three of the university security guards that entered the hall. They didn't seem to notice any of us sitting at our desks, but rather headed straight for the head invigilator. I started to try to prepare myself to return to the exam, waiting for the head invigilator to tell us that it was inevitably somebody's poor sense of humour that led to a false alarm being set off during finals week.

Security moved to the front with a megaphone. "Attention. At this time we would like to ask all of you to calmly return to your dorms or place of residence. We will escort you to each dorm building or the parking lot. Please follow the security officer holding the appropriate sign to be escorted. Thank you for your co-operation.

There was a murmur, but everyone obeyed, including me. I even found myself whispering to the girl next to me who I despise. Not that either of us were a well of information.

I saw dark clouds in the distance, as we walked to our buildings. "What is happening?" I whispered, eyes fixed on the clouds.

I sat at my desk in my dorm room, staring at Ashley's empty bed and chair.

"Is someone attacking us? No. Nobody could hit us from that way. Another Chernobyl? Only here? Maybe they can't stop this one. Or maybe those irritating geeks online are right and a supervolcano erupted. Would have to be one of those two, or something I can't even think of." I glanced at a picture of Dylan and me on my desk, his smiling face lost in my hair. "I need to get home. Mom and Dylan might be in trouble."

I left my laptop bag and pulled all my clothes out of the drawers. I stuffed a tank top, blouse, cardigan into the bag. Changing from my skirt and blouse out for a pair of jeans and a tank top. I pulled the blanket off my bed, and stuff it in too, as well as the flashlight I keep in my drawer.

I lifted my bag, and moved toward the door, my hand stopped on the doorknob. The black cloud loomed in my mind. "Filter." I grabbed my blouse with the finest weave, and my favourite green blouse. I hesitated to cut it with my scissors, but manage to bring myself too. Layering the fabric I make it into a makeshift handkerchief like you'd see in a spaghetti western on a bandit. I put this around my neck and rushed out.

A group of girls was in our common kitchen, including Ashley, our R.A. trying to calm them down but her voice is lost in the chatter.

I slipped in unnoticed, grabbing as much perishable food as I had in my cupboard. Mostly soup, instant noodles, and Kraft dinners. I also pulled a knife out of the drawer, my longest and sharpest knife with a serrated edge, that came with a real leather sheath.

The R.A. noticed me go, but was too busy with the girls to care.

```
Lily,    12:43 p.m.
```

I was sitting in the library when it happened. It was finals week, and I was preparing to take my exams by spending most of my time with my head in various books. When it started, I barely noticed it. If I had been concentrating any more on my Engineering book, I would have missed it. The whole building seemed to shiver by just the tiniest amount. I looked up from the table to see if anyone else had noticed the small tremor. It was pretty clear that they had. Everyone was looking around at each other, as if any of us may have had answers as to what was going on.

I knew then that there was a chance that something big had happened. I slowly walked to the front doors of the library. As I looked out through the glass on the front of the building I saw people, my fellow students, all standing still with their eyes on the sky looking at something just behind the library. I had to get outside to see what everyone was so interested in.

As I stepped outside and away from the building, people started to run and shout at each other. I couldn't understand what they were saying, but I was more worried about what was behind the library anyway. About a hundred feet away from the building I looked back, and I saw immediately why everyone was rushing around me. The sky over the horizon was dark grey, and it was growing darker. It was as if the biggest, darkest storm you could imagine was speeding towards us. It was moving unnaturally quickly. It couldn't have been a normal storm cloud, and I knew that storms didn't cause earthquakes anyway. Whatever this was, it was dangerous and I needed to move.

I ran into the nearest building, which was the Student Union, and it was even more full of rushing and shouting people than the sidewalk outside had been. I made my way to the edge of the room, away from the panicking people. There, I saw an image I will never forgot. On a small, flat screen television in the corner, the news was playing an emergency update. The screen was plastered with images of dark skies and buildings that had cracked or collapsed from the shaking ground. I reached for the television and turned the volume as high as it would go. The people around started to slow down, and some even stopped to listen to the broadcast with me.

The anchor woman on the television spoke in a calm voice, but my nerves were already frayed beyond repair.

"If you are just joining us, " she said from behind the desk of the newsroom, "the supervolcano beneath Yellowstone Park has just erupted. Stay inside, find shelter, and if you must go outside cover your nose and mouth."

I looked through a nearby window and could see the huge cloud of what I now assumed must have been ash moving closer and closer. There was still some sunlight, but that wouldn't last long.

"The oncoming ash cloud is not safe to breathe", warned the news woman. I would need to find shelter soon or I would certainly be stuck in this storm.

"New information!" a shout came from behind me. I turned around and just over the crowd of people that had gathered around the television I could see a woman standing on a table with a small radio to her ear.

"The government is saying to leave the city. The cloud isn't breathable. We have to leave." The woman on the table was not nearly as calm and collected as the woman on the news, and her nervous voice seemed to stir the crowd into a frenzy. We were receiving mixed messages from the news, and nobody really knew what was going on. All I knew was that I wanted to get home, and I needed a ride.

I pulled my phone from my pocket and went back outside where there was less noise. The cloud was even closer now, but I still had time to dial Annabelle's number. I checked that I had a signal and put the phone to my ear.

A busy signal was all that I could hear. I had to keep trying, so I decided to dial Marcus, who would likely be with Annabelle anyway because they were so close. I put the phone to my ear again and Marcus answered after the first ring.

"Lily, " he said with a comforting mixture of surprise and relief, "Where are you, are you alright?"

"I'm fine. I'm alright. I'm in front of the Student Union. Do you have any idea what's going on?" I asked him, hoping he knew more than I did.

Sadly, he said, "No. The people on the radios are saying something about a super volcano, but I thought it was an earthquake, not a volcano."

"I know, I know, " I responded, "Where are you, and where is Annabelle? We need to get together."

"I'm in the dorms, and Annabelle and Maria are here with me. Maria's car has five seats in it. You should ride with us. We're going to get supplies and try to run away from this."

His offer was all I could have asked for. "Yes. I'll be there in just a minute. Wait for me, " I said as I hung up. I ran as quickly as my feet would carry me.

Mrs.Gallie and Dylan,   1:15 p.m.

The call from the school had been unexpected. It wasn't often that Dylan's school closed early.

They told me that there was some incident elsewhere and that they felt safer sending the kids home. When I did pick him up all Dylan could talk about was how they had been let out early, as if I didn't realize that that was what was going on.

"We were painting when Mrs. Barnes came in, " he told me excitedly.

"Oh? That's one of the assistant teachers, isn't it?", I asked, not really caring for an answer.

"Yeah, Mrs. Barnes is the assistant teacher. She came in to talk to Mrs. Dean. I didn't hear what she said, but she was probably telling her that school was closing, " he explained to me.

Before I had gone to pick Dylan up from school, I had turned on the television to see if there was any news about what was going on. What I had seen was awful. There were storms, huge clouds, volcanoes, and earthquakes. Someone might think it looked like the end of the world. I didn't mention any of this to Dylan, of course, but I did refrain from turning on the radio as we rode home just in case the news was on there as well.

Dylan looked up at me and smiled as he continued, "That's when Mrs. Dean told us that school was closing. Do you think it'll be closed forever? They said that you would come and pick us up, but I wanted to keep painting."

The roads were becoming more congested the longer we were in the car. There were people running from house to house, and a few were shouting down the streets. Dylan didn't notice at all. He was far too busy telling me every detail of what had happened since school had closed.

"After I finished my painting, I washed my hands, and Mrs. Barnes came back in and talked to Mrs. Dean again. They talk a lot. Then Mrs. Dean told us to get our backpacks and go in the hall. We got to sit in the hall until you came."

"I even got to sit next to Thomas and Matthew. Can they come over next week?" He looked at me expectantly.

"Maybe honey, if the weather is nice, " I told him. The truth was that his talking comforted me. Even if I didn't pay attention to every word of it, just knowing that he was safe beside me, with everyone outside losing their minds, made me feel better.

"That's when you came to pick me up, " he continued with his story. I let him ramble on for a few more minutes. The traffic was such a nightmare that it was taking us at least twice as long to get home as it normally did.

When he eventually asked me if we were home yet, I told him that we were nearly there, and he leaned back against the seat of the car and looked out his window.

After a moment of his not talking I looked into the back seat to make sure he was still okay. He was staring up into the sky with the look of a curious child. I leaned forward and looked up through the windshield. Just over the trees, to the northwest, the sky had begun to go grey. There was a huge bank of clouds there that I hadn't seen before. I crossed my fingers that the storms that they had mentioned on the news were not coming towards us.

When we finally pulled into our driveway, I let Dylan out of the car we went inside the house. The sunlight was slowly fading so I let Dylan play with his toys on the living room floor. I went to the phone to call one of the neighbors and see if they knew more about what was going on. Every number I called got a busy signal. That's when I decided that I needed to turn the radio on, and really listen to what was happening. When I heard the man from the station say the words "Yellowstone supervolcano" I knew that this was not just bad weather, and it was not going to go away.

The Ward Family,   1:23 p.m.

Every car that could possibly pour into the

city that afternoon seemed to be trying to do so. The traffic hadn't stopped, but it moved far slower than it normally did. Boxed in by big SUV's driven by suburban housewives, sat a mother and her son in a smaller white family car. The boy was happily playing with a large yellow dump truck in the back seat, whilst the mother tapped the steering wheel impatiently. She wasn't aware how heavily she was tapping until she accidentally hit the horn. Her expression changed to one of embarrassment, but she relaxed slightly as cars behind her joined in. As she settled back into her worry, her son called from the back seat, "Storm." Looking to the sky she saw that between the strips of horizon visible through the office block buildings was a continuous banner of black clouds forming across the sky. She decided to praise the child's identification, but they seemed darker and thicker than normal. After a while and having to fight her way to the side of the road, the mother got out of the car, collected her son from the back seat, and started towards the school building.

The small playground was saturated with worried parents, all responding to the flustered secretary informing them that the school would unexpectedly have to close early. Her youngest daughter had been attending the school for several years, yet she recognised none of the faces of other parents from PTA meetings, or sports days. She stood waiting, occasionally looking up at the sky watching the approaching darkness.

The children were released in a naive wave. There was the usual happy, screaming noise of the end of school, magnified by the fact that it was early and the prospect that school might be cancelled for a few days. A girl approached the woman, babbling about all the things that she was planning to do if they never had to go to school again. She would watch T.V. forever and only eat cake, and she would get a cat and play with it and she would become a world famous artist.

Grabbing her hand, her mother sighed and hurried them out of the school gate struggling through the crowds of other parents and children.

The traffic was worse away from the school where, in addition to other parents, there were people leaving work and trying to hurry home, and people trying to get back to family elsewhere. The cloud was getting thicker and closer, but it was staying fairly high up.

Outside the town there was less traffic and the roads were straighter and the journey quicker. She parked in front of a large Victorian house. Her husband wasn't home yet, nor was her eldest daughter, but she had been informed that the school was closing, and the buses were still in service.

She pulled her top up over her mouth, and then used her cardigan to cover her son's face as she hurried him into the house. Her daughter copied her, and they quickly shuffled up the stairs, over the porch, and inside.

"Lola, Chris, stay in the living room, I need to ring Daddy." The mother called as she wandered into the kitchen to grab the phone, dialing the number as she leant against the wall where she could watch the children, praying the line wasn't busy. He picked up after a few seconds.

"Rich, the girls have both been sent home from school. . . No, they aren't ill. Have you not looked outside, there is a massive cloud, ash they think it is. . . Lola's home, I picked her up. Millie's on the bus, they were still on their way. You know what they are like. . . You should come home too. . . No, she'll already be on the bus. . . Go to the store on your way back Get as much as you can. . . If I am being paranoid then laugh at me later, but right now please do it, just in case. . . Humour me Rich."

While his mother was distracted by the phone the little boy, Chris, had climbed up onto the coffee table and started shouting, "I'm the King of the castle." The glass wobbled, and the vase of flowers on top of it teetered. It was an impractical vase, too narrow at the bottom. It was only art Mr Wards parents had come round the night before. It was a wedding gift that his mother liked to see being used, and they didn't like to annoy his mother. It fell onto the carpet with a thud. Chris looked to his mother sheepishly, and she sighed.

"I have to go Chris knocked that blasted vase over, I need to go clear it up, " she continued to the phone receiver, "Hurry up and get home Rich, but after you've been to the shop I love you too Yes, see you later."

1:45 p.m.

The bank was filled with the noise of typing and computer clicking. Money moved in and out between accounts across the globe.

"Can I set up this payment please, the ex-wife has asked for more money." A portly man in a pinstriped suit strolled in and grumbled, shoving a scrap of paper and his card under the glass.

"Certainly, Sir." The cashier smiled weakly

and clicked with her mouse.

"Can I please put this money into my account." A little boy asked, his mother standing behind him. As the child stretched to see over the counter holding up some money, his mother warned him not to drop his savings book.

"Of course. Wow, that is a lot of money, where did you get it all?" The cashier took it through the little gap in the bottom of the protective screen and counted up the $30.

"It was his birthday, last week." His mother smiled, stepping forwards and brushing a small bit of fuzz out of his hair. "We wanted to get it put in before it gets lost."

"Ah, how old are you now then?"

"5, and 3 days." The child beamed.

There was the general Monday chit-chat between the two cashiers when things quieted down, in the lull just before lunch time, when businesses decided people could take down cheques as they went out for food and coffee: "How was your weekend?", "How was dinner at your mother-in-laws?", "Oh me and Dan saw it on date night last week, what about that ending?".

Both of the cashiers had customers when the system went down. One was transferring $2000 for a business, "I'm sorry Sir, the system appears to have crashed. What I'll do is write you out a receipt and I'll make sure I give you a call when I've logged back in to keep you updated on its progress." The other was transferring money for a woman paying for her mother's flights from Alaska. "If it hasn't gone through I can always send it later, don't worry too much."

The manager was just leaving for lunch. One of the women called him back, and he fiddled and clicked and typed, but the screen kept telling him "The connection has been lost. Trying to reconnect." It was unsuccessful. He tried to ring a neighbouring branch and after it rang and rang and rang he received an apology saying:

"Due to unforeseen circumstance we will be unable to make transactions over the phone, in person, or online until further notice."

On the other side of the country, in the bank's head office, chaos had descended. The banking system was in totally collapse. A senior member was trying to get in touch with various branches to see if it was just a problem with their computers. He couldn't get through. The TV no longer worked. Remembering one of the janitors had a pocket radio, and a few frantic minutes of internal phone calls he managed to track him down and get him to come to his office. Following a couple of minutes of trying to explain in broken spanish that he wanted to borrow the janitors radio, and a few minutes of drawing, he managed to get what he needed. It didn't take him too long to find a broadcast. Through the tiny headphones he heard:

"BREAKING NEWS: Worst Economic Crisis in Decades." Through a hail of static he could just about make out the words Wall Street... in London, Paris, Tokyo... System failure... initiated in America, causing share prices to fall.

In the moments of disbelief that came after he

heard the man on the radio describe the result-
ing public panic, buying food, water, and supplies. The police had to been called to numerous
riots. He paused for a moment to think of his
own family, and hopes that there cupboards are
full enough to weather what ever this storm was.

1:50 p.m.

The students stared at the algebra on the board
with vague interest. Some of them already knew
it, there were others who continued scribbling out
their workings when it didn't come up to the right
answer, and others were completely lost.

"Letters are for English, numbers are for math,
why mix them up, "the boy two seats from the

front complained; he had won the poetry competition last year. Another struggling at the back complained that, seeing as she didn't want to be a rocket scientist, why was any of this relevant. The teacher just shook her head a bit and continued to move round the class helping those not managing and setting more revision for those who had already finished. She reached a girl clicking her pen and avoiding the teachers attention by hiding behind her hair.

"Try page 44." The teacher moved promptly on to the next teen getting grumpy in the heat.

The girl fumbled with her textbook, knocking her pen onto the floor. Her friend passed it back to her with a smile, and she mouthed, "Thanks" to him. She hadn't even written down the page number or the title of the page, when another teacher hurried in and gestured for theirs to join him outside. The class burst into noise, some students cursing algebra, others wondered what the teachers could be discussing outside, the normal suspects came up with the normal responses: there was a fight, there had been an accident, maybe they were kissing. Some just chatted among themselves.

"Class, quiet." Their teacher looked anxious as she walked back into the room. "Put your books away, and put your things in your bags. If your parent would normally pick you up please go to the sports hall and wait for them to arrive. They have or will be called and told to come to get you. If you normally take the bus, please make your way to the bus stop now, they will be leaving in fifteen minutes. This early release is only a precaution, so I would like you to continue to prepare for your exams, and I shall see you tomorrow. A day off is no excuse for laziness."

The students looked at each other with puzzled expressions, one piped up "What's going on Mrs. Landy?" The teacher just told him to go to the hall to wait for his mother.

The girl stood and shrugged at her friend.

"Shall we head to the bus then?" He said as they shuffled towards the door with others.

"I need to get my violin from the music room."
She replied

"Okay, we have time. That should only take
two minutes, right?"

"Sure." They headed off at a fast pace, grabbed
the instrument, and then joined the throngs of
students being herded towards the bus stop or the
hall.

The normal pushing and shoving occurred as
everyone tried to pile onto the buses and get the
seats at the back. The girl sat awkwardly in a
double seat, bag squished between her and the
metal side as she hugged her violin to her chest.
Her friend leant over to open the window and release the stuffy air, before slumping into the seat
next to her.

"Did you hear the noise earlier? The rumbling
when we were in biology?" He turned to her.

"They must have finally taken down the old
apartment block." She shrugged leaning on the
top of the case.

"You think they've got rid of all the squatters?" He frowned at her.

"They must have. It explains the dust, maybe that's why we got sent home?"

"Maybe." He suddenly didn't seem so interested.

"Are you up to much later?" He said as they approached his stop.

"I'll be online after I've practised." She turned to look out the window as he stood and left.

The bus moved away, but the traffic was getting denser, as was the grey dust in the air. The cars had to turn their lights on and were using their horns more than in a normal rush hour. People were hurrying from shop to shop, some were running. Cardigans and jackets, light scarves, and whatever else people seemed to have with them were being used to cover mouths and noses, and others were using sunglasses to protect their eyes. People walked slowly in the diminishing visibility, bumping into each other. An elderly woman was shoved over by someone running down the street. The bus was stationary for a good five minutes, and it started to creep forward before anybody helped her.

The bus moved along the route stopping less and less frequently. The girl was the last one on the bus, but outside the window the scene was the same. If anything, the panic seemed to be getting worse, she saw someone physically push a child out of their way and nearly into the road. The bus driver rolled his eyes and muttered that things were going to the dogs and that it was despicable.

"Your stop dear. Get home safely." The bus driver called back. He wasn't as cheery as normal, but she thanked him all the same as she stepped off to walk the 300 yards down the track to her house.

2:00 p.m.

Papers littered the floor, blown off the top of stacks as people crossed paths on their way to her and there. One of the perks of being such a senior figure in the bank was the proximity of his offices the elevators. He'd worked over the duration of his whole career to get close and closer, using his long commutes from lift to desk earlier on in his career to remind himself just what he was working to get to.

A couple of minutes earlier he had received a call, through his personal secretary, from his panicked wife asking if he could make his way home immediately. Whilst she sounded worried about the cloud of ash, she had not used their safety word, an unfortunate necessity for the families of top level employees of the bank, to ensure the containment of what had broadly been referred to as incidents. Another positive of being such an established member of staff was that his key card gave him lift priority, which would fast track the lift to his floor, by passing any lower requests. He was pleased to see that all the staff had remembered their extensive training, and had reverted to their cell phones, rather than making family calls on the company's phones.

When the building had been built the security company had complained about high level executives traveling down the side of the building, however, today it offered him his first view of the cloud of ash that had cut through the skyline.

The journey from the 30th floor only took fifty seconds, a purposeful design to give the banks prospective customers the impression that the bank was a quick and efficient company that they wanted to do business with. When the doors opened on the ground floor he left the lift, in awe of what he'd just seen in the sky, that he'd forgotten that he'd wanted to request the basement car park. Before he could remedy this the lift had started to climb back up the building. On opening the doorway to the staircase he instantly remembered why everybody took the lift.

In the cool of the underground carpark, people walked towards their cars, avoiding each other and already moving cars with brake lights flashing.

"Ward." His boss yelled across the car park. "Provided phones still work, I'll let you know when we start again. Shouldn't be too long, the cloud will just blow away, I don't know what everyone is worrying about."

"Sure." Mr Ward replied, rolling his eyes as he walked away. There was working in a bank and then there was being a heartless banker.

After moving a jerry can and bike pump from the flatbed of his trunk he got into his car, sighed and leant back. There was plenty of room for as much as he could get, so Liv could stop nagging him. He hoped she wouldn't worry too much, and anyway it would be nice to spend time with the children without the fuss of Christmas or thanksgiving, and it would be pleasant to escape his boss for a little. He had been particularly tedious this week.

Joining the lines of honking traffic, the car crawled out of the car park. Outside the street lights glowed eerily; the sky was a thick grey colour.

The cloud had come in quicker than he had expected but, someone in the office and mentioned that it was getting darker, and lower. He began to understand his wife's panic. A school bus was in the next lane, he looked up almost expecting to see his daughter, then shook himself, it would be ridiculous for her bus to be in the city, it would mean that it would be going in completely the wrong direction.

Tamie,   2:05 p.m.

I needed to call my mother and brother. Home was probably the safest place to be right now, and even though it would probably take me time to get there, I needed to let them know that I was on my way. I pulled my phone out of my nearly empty backpack. The screen lit up at my touch and told me that it was early afternoon. I had no way to know whether or not my brother would still be at school or whether my mom would have her phone with her. I checked that I still had a signal and dialed her up anyway. My heart dropped a bit when all I got was a busy signal. I realized just a few moments later that with all of the chaos going on outside, phone lines would probably be too busy to use for the rest of the day.

Even though I wasn't able to speak with them, I still knew I had to get home somehow. So, I left my room, locked the door, and made my way downstairs and out the front door. I needed to get to my car and get away from this place.

The campus security guards were clearly having trouble keeping everyone calm. The few officers that were left on campus were pointing and shouting at some students, and breaking up fights between others. The students seemed to have riled themselves into a frenzied mob and were beginning to destroy things. It was as if the security guards were trying to mop up a rain storm.

As I made my way towards the parking lot I felt my backpack, light on my shoulders. If I was going to make the trip all the way down to Texas, it would likely take me a while, and there probably wouldn't be many places to get food along the way. I needed to stock up if I was going to make the journey.

One of the campus cafeterias was close by, so I decided to duck in for a moment and pick up what canned and dried goods I could before I went to my car. Although the foreboding cloud was still a ways off, the cafeteria building looked as if it had been hit by a tornado in the last hour. The doors were closed and secured with a metal bar, but getting in was as easy as climbing through the busted out windows instead.

Broken glass crunched under my feet as I made my way towards the shelves of food. Other people were jumping over counters, knocking down furniture, and breaking whatever they could get their hands on, but I was only after the things

I needed. I wasn't there for senseless violence. The first food that I found was some fresh fruit. I grabbed enough for a few days, but I knew it would go bad quickly so I decided to go for more long lasting options.

As I walked among the rows of candy bars, junk food, and frozen pizza, I couldn't help but see all of the other people, both students and not, running through the cafeteria. I caught a glimpse of a few as they shouted and jumped on each other heading from one side of the building to the other. Some of them held makeshift weapons and baseball bats in their hands. The university had fallen into anarchy. With darkness on the horizon and nothing to be done about it, people seemed to have decided complete destruction was the only thing left for them.

I pulled a few bottles of water from the coolers that lined one wall. I knew they wouldn't stay cool for long in the hot summer weather, so I took a quick drink from one while it was still fresh. The cold water traced an icy line down my throat and calmed my mind a bit. I grabbed a few more provisions, just enough to fill the rest of my bag, and started to make my way out of the cafeteria.

As I was climbing back through the broken window on my way outside, two figures blocked my way. A man and woman, clearly other students, were standing only a few feet in front of me.

"What have you got there, " sneered the man.

"Stolen food, no doubt. Thief, " spat the woman, accusingly. I backed up a few steps, but for each inch I retreated they moved closer to me. I knew I still had my pepper spray. I had put it in the front pocket of my bag before I left my room, but to get to it I would have to take the bag off and reach into the pocket. I started to slowly, carefully slip the bag off my shoulder.

Without warning, the woman lunged at me shouting, "Give it to me!"

I swung the bag around, and it connected solidly with the side of her face. Thankful that I had grabbed enough cans to make the bag heavy, I pulled the pepper spray out and pointed it towards the man.

He looked back and forth between me and his friend that was now laying on the ground. "You bitch, " he hissed, and started towards me again.

I sprayed him directly in the eyes with the can of pepper spray. He screeched, and in his blindness tripped over his accomplice.

I quickly got as far from both of them as I could. I slung my bag over my shoulder and ran to the parking lot in search of my car.

Radio Broadcast,   2:45 p.m.

The ash cloud generated by the volcano at Yellowstone has reduced visibility across the United States. It is impossible to fly safely and even walking at ground level can be hazardous.

Anything that is done outside of a safe place will be deadly.

Food is likely to become scarce. Fresh produce will eventually be impossible to come by and canned food for those affected by the cloud could well become a rare luxury.

This means that civil unrest is likely to break out soon. Riots and looting are certain to take place in urban areas, possibly worse than those in Detroit in 67.

Widespread panic and destruction will follow. That is all for now.

[static]

Lily,   2:46 p.m.

I had made it to Marcus's dorm, seeing that he, Annabelle and Maria were safe. . That was a relief, because it seemed that most of the campus had begun to lose its mind. People were scrambling and shouting everywhere I looked. We got into Maria's car and decided to make a quick trip to the store for whatever food and supplies we could find. Wherever we were going, it was going to take us a while to get to where we were going.

We drove up to the nearest supermarket. I was absolutely shocked at the chaos that was teeming through the building. What had once been a civil business was now a free-for-all with people climbing over one another to take whatever provisions they could manage to get their hands on. We all decided to get in and get out of the store as quickly as we could. I managed to grab some bottles of water, a couple boxes of cereal, and a couple of cans of soup. Together we grabbed enough food to last us for a few days. With the trunk of the car full, we drove as carefully as we could out of town. The roads were busy and slow moving, but we eventually made our way onto the highway.

"Do we know where we're going ?" asked Marcus. He had insisted on driving despite the fact that the car was Maria's. She didn't protest as Marcus was a good driver and liked to be control when in a car. In a stressful situation like this, the last thing anybody wanted would be an exacerbant.

"No, we have no where to go, " Annabelle replied in a defeatist tone.

"My grandma lives in Texas. If we could somehow make our way there, we could stay with her, " I offered. I was shocked that Marcus didn't have a destination. His parents lived in a nearby state, but I wasn't sure exactly which one. Marcus didn't talk about his parents often, and I assumed that was part of why he chose not to return to them.

"Any other ideas?" He paused to give us a chance to think of any. After a minute or two of silence, he said, "Lilly's grandmothers it is then." Marcus decided.

"We need gas, " Marcus said, worried, "I hope the stations haven't been emptied."

Abandoned cars were strewn along the road. No sign of damage or collision. They were likely passers by who had been in our situation only hours or minutes earlier.

We continued to drive at a much slower pace, since the path we had to follow was no longer straight.

"Why do you think these cars have been left?" Maria asked of no one in particular.

"Car failure, ran out of gas..." Marcus took a few guesses.

Maria offered, "Can we not just syphon gas from one of these abandoned cars?"

"No maria, that's against the law, " I responded.

She raised her eyebrows at me and responded, "Lily, these cars have been abandoned. Finders keepers..."

"Losers weepers" Annabelle finished her sentence. They then high fived. It was like we were on a family outing and they were two annoying sisters sitting in the back seat of the car.

Marcus turned to me, "They have a point".

" Fine, " I sighed. I didn't find the idea of stealing someone's gas appealing. They might have parked the car only to return to it later. I didn't see much point in protesting. When these guys had an idea they ran with it.

Marcus pulled the car to a stop. "Stay here while I go to search." He left the car and pulled out what seemed like gas can and a pipe.

"Sheeesh he's prepared, " Annabelle said, surprised.

"He's Marcus, " I reminded her, "You know he's always thinking ahead."

"Yeah Annabelle, it's like you don't even know know him" teased Maria.

They could be pretty annoying.

Maria and Annabelle babbled on as I began to worry about my grandmother. Since I'd moved to university her mobility had begun to decline. I felt guilty enough leaving her behind to pursue my dreams, but she had insisted. Could this have cost her life?

Marcus returned and fed the car it's much needed sustenance, snapping me out of my anxious thoughts. He sat in the driver's seat with a concerned look on his face.

"What's wrong?"I pried.

"It's distressing to think that families have had to flee their homes. The car next to us has two booster seats in the back"

I had no reply. We just continued to drive. It was all we could do.

3:12 p.m.

I remained with Dylan in the kitchen, I had my arm around his shoulder which comforted us both. "What reading have you got for us this week sweetheart", I tried to take his mind off from worrying about his sister by asking him to show me this weeks reading he had been given from school. If anything, this was largely for my own sake. I tried to convince myself that she would be fine; that she had bunked up with some friends and would wait out the duration of this entire event, or perhaps she had even managed to get away from campus and was indeed on her way home.

"It's about space men", Dylan's enthusiasm cut into my thought process, he was always very good at doing this, and it was much welcome.

"Oh wow", I exclaimed, "Are they traveling to Mars?"

"They're on a Moon base, watching over Earth", he continued to explain, "look at those".

Dylan pointed to a water colour illustration of the space men' watering plants in a greenhouse with a view of the Earth.

I smiled at the drawing with Dylan, "we should

have a greenhouse like that one", he announced.

We were soon interrupted by the ringing of a car alarm outside the back of the house in the street behind. Dylan looked up in distress wondering what was going on, as did I, which came as a shock as I saw my reflection in the window.

Looking outside the ash cloud had massed around the house. The further away you attempted to look the darkness of the cloud thickened. The garden no longer existed, you could just about see the flower pots against the fence, but the landscape had been consumed by ash.

Grey specks were hitting the window with some force and I knew that it wouldn't be long before looking out of the window became a sheer impossibility.

"How long is the weather going to be like this for?" My shoulder slid off from Dylan's shoulder as I moved to turn on the radio; which sat on the counter in the far side of the kitchen, in an attempt to cover up the echos of the car alarm.

Wailing static was the only program on air, so

I quickly turned it off.

"I don't know dear, hopefully it'll pass over soon", I eventually replied, dismayed by the static on the radio. Hopping that I had turned it off without disturbing him, but knowing that I had already failed. No doubt the ash was affecting the radio reception. I probably should have known this upon reflection, but I can't blame myself for being hopeful.

"But I think we may be stuck in it for some time".

"I don't like it", Dylan looked out of the window, he was always curious. Always exploring and now he was trapped with his mother, and surrounded by a void of ash and shadows.

"I'm here Dylan, tell you what if you promise that you'll be brave for me, I'll be brave for you", I held out my hand for Dylan to shake, thinking that I was a cool mom, before wondering whether people still said cool.

Dylan looked at my open hand and smiled, he shook it with a firm grip, "Deal".

I was a cool mom.

Dylan looked down back at the space men in his book, he turned the page looking at a space family' eating extravagant food on the surface of the Moon. The family had a checkered red and white picnic cloth and a wicker basket which held food that looked more like stalagmites rather than that of food.

"Look at it this way, at least you don't have school for the next few days".

Dylan smiled, the small gaps in his teeth we're charming as if he were returning the reassurance.

The car alarm finally came to a stop.

"Finally", I announced. Dylan shared in my rejoice by yelling a large hooray at the closure of car alarm symphony. I moved back over towards the radio and took a look inside the kitchen cupboards. Wondering what we would do for tea, and hoping that the electricity wouldn't be too badly affected by the ash cloud. I had no doubt that it would, it was more a matter of time.

Dylan continued to look through the pictures

of the book the school had given him.

"This could be me and Tamie", he announced.

I turned around to see him holding up the book of a young boy and girl in space suits playing a game of catch in space."

"As soon as she gets back, you could go on a holiday to space together".

"How will we get there?" Dylan looked puzzled by such a suggestion.

"Well you're going to have to build a rocket aren't you?" I explained, designing a project to entertain him.

"Tamie will be okay won't she?" I should have predicted that it wouldn't take long before he began to worry again.

"Hey, Tamie will be fine. I bet Tamie's making her way home, she'll be back in no time. What you should be asking is Will I be able to build my rocket before Tamie returns?' Tamie will be here soon and then we'll all go to space.

"Do you think that she'll be okay in the storm?"

Dylan's question, was one I did not want to

consider, if she was at the university; how badly had the ash cloud hit? And if she was traveling home. The storm was not worth thinking about, I am here with Dylan and I promised to be brave.

I turned back to the cupboard and wondered about omelet for tea, we still had a few of eggs left. "You know, if were to do just as well as Tamie is, we'll have to pop out and get some food sooner or later".

Dylan looked up at me curious.

"You and me kid, we'll be great".

4:35 p.m.

The cupboards were bordering on bare that morning. We had some food that would last us a couple of days, if we were careful maybe three or four, but no longer than that. The reality of the situation hit me hard: soon we would not be able to feed ourselves. I began to wonder how other families had managed, or whether anyone else was still occupying the local area besides Dylan and I. I knew families who had gone to other relatives, or had left with the hope of trying to escape the ash. I had to venture into the ash cloud and find whatever food I could.

It would be hard. Spending too long in the ash would have a severe consequences with my asthma, but if I didn't Dylan would starve. I decided that I would leave him at home. If the ash was bad for my health, I had to protect him from similar troubles.

Dylan was in his room where he was happily dancing in circles with his favorite teddy bear, Sebastian. I needed to tell him that I was going out, but I didn't want him to worry about me.

"Dylan, sweetie, mommy needs to go to the store, " I said as pleasantly as I could. I wanted him to think of it as any other day.

"Okay, I'll get my shoes on, " he said putting his bear back on his bed.

I kneeled down in front of him. "No, no, sweetie. I'm afraid it's just Mommy who's going to the store. You'll get to stay home by yourself like a big boy today."

His eyes grew big with excitement as he exclaimed, "Really? I promise I'll be good."

"Okay. You know the rules. Stay out of the kitchen, and don't open the door for anyone." I reminded him, hoping that he would understand the gravity of my words.

"I know Mommy, I know, " he said pushing me towards the door. He was so ready to be a big boy, but he couldn't possibly have understood how important this was to me.

Standing at the front door, I grabbed a scarf to wrap around my mouth and nose to keep the ash out of my lungs. I checked that my inhaler was in my pocket as well, just in case. With the scarf firmly around my face, I took one more look back at Dylan, waved, and stepped outside.

The air outside was thick with dust and warm with the oncoming summer heat. Even though it should have been the middle of the day, it was dim outside with the ash blocking out most of the sun's rays. I tried to breath in the dry, dusty air, but my lungs protested. Every breath felt dry and my lungs panicked. My shoulders shook with the effort, and I took a moment to calm myself. I pulled out my inhaler, but didn't use. I took slow breaths as I balanced the small device in my hand. I didn't need it. I couldn't afford for it to run out.

After a moment of focusing on steadying my breath, I was steady enough to walk. I started to make my way to the supermarket that I knew was only a little over a mile away. At first, I had almost hoped to meet other people going about their lives. I hoped that perhaps someone could tell me more about what was going on. I hoped for some help or a friendly face, but then I considered why other people might be outside like me. Most people were probably running low on food just like we were. That meant that anyone I met out here in the grey, dark streets would be competing for the same food that I needed to keep my child alive. I decided then that other people were best to be avoided. I would get what I needed and get home before someone wandered into my home, to my son, in their own quest for resources.

I finally made it to the front doors of the store. The store was dark through the glass. I hadn't been expecting it to be up and running, but I had at least hoped for it to look similar to how it had. Instead, it looked like something out of a zombie movie. Some shelves were tipped over. There was vegetables on the ground. It seemed empty of life. I walked through the gaping front entrance where the doors were barely hanging onto their frames. Once inside, I was able to lower the scarf from my face and gave myself a minute to just cough and breath in the slightly cleaner air of the store.

I spent at least an hour wandering up and down the rows of empty shelves grabbing anything

I could find that we could eat. I ended up with a few cans of beans, a large box of crackers, some cereal, and a few packages of dried meats. It would be enough for a few days. Then I remembered the half empty inhaler in my pocket and looked to the back of the store where there was a small pharmacy.

I made my way to the pharmacy counter picking up a couple of small first aid kits and bottles of aspirin as I went. At the counter, I paused, hoping by some miracle that there would be a knowledgeable pharmacist waiting for me to tell them what I needed. I knew there wasn't anyone like that left in this store, so I slid myself over the counter instead. I looked across shelf and shelf for the familiar blue box that held the inhalers that I needed. After a few sweeps of the lables I was sure that what I needed wasn't here. I resigned myself to using my inhaler less, and I promised I wouldn't tell Dylan because it would only worry him more and he could do nothing to help me.

I left the store and made it home without incident. It was a long walk though, and my bag had gotten heavy. By the time I made it back to my front door my lungs were screaming for relief from the thick, dry, and ashy air. I coughed and wheezed, and finally I decided I needed another breath from my inhaler to steady myself before greeting Dylan. I puffed the cold medication into my lungs, breathed deep, and stepped inside.

Dylan immediately ran up to me saying, "How did I do mommy? I didn't go in the kitchen at all, and I was all by myself. I was a big boy, right?"

"Yes dear, you did very well, " I reassured him as I unloaded my bag of food into the cupboards. "Let's go into the living room and sit down."

He followed me into the next room, and we sat in the middle of the floor where he had already had a puzzle laid out. I sat in silence as he told me all about his day at home alone. His voice calmed me even as my lungs continued to burn.

5:30 p.m.

I looked down at the small scraps that we'd been able to find at the local store. Those rioters had certainly done a good job at stripping it bare, a couple of dented tins of beans, and a few disfigured packets of Kraft Mac 'n' Cheese. I hoped to have found something a bit fresher at the local shop, but even the back store room had been ravaged. The lack of fresh dairy was also frustrating. I knew that what I had left in the fridge was very limited, in both amount and time that it would be safe to feed to Dylan. With this in mind I decided that it would be best to have mac and cheese and hope that I could find some more milk somewhere soon. When I came home, I filled the kettle and set it to boil and placed a clean saucepan on the burners, and poured the powdered cheese mixture in. I felt the fine dust particles catch the back of my throat. Coughing, I cursed my asthma, and quickly had to take my inhaler from my back pocket, and take a deep breath. For a few moments I just had to stand there as Dylan contently colours at the table. Before putting the inhaler back in my pocket I quickly checked to see how many doses I had left, not enough for the way that I was using it. When I felt like the worst has passed I took the milk from the fridge, only to realise whilst measuring that there isn't quite enough to fulfil the recipe on the back of the packet. I had to top it up with some water from the tap. I looked at the dented tin of hotdog sausages, I knew how much Dylan likes mac and cheese with hot dogs in it, but I decided we could not afford this luxury. Going by how empty the local store was, I didn't like to think about the stock resources of the ones around it.

Dylan was drawn to the kitchen by the smell of the dinner crisping under the grill. Knowing the answer he asked what was for tea, but his face fell when I told him that there would be an absence of hot dogs. He still offered to help set the table, so I placed the chipped plates and warm cutlery on the table and let him move it into the correct place, whilst I toasted a few bits of bread to add some more substance.

Dylan sat and waited for me to join him. We sat opposite each other on the family table. He tucked in almost as soon as I picked up my fork. He must have been hungry, because it was gone before I was halfway through mine. He sat there chewing on his crust, staring past me and out the window.

"Mom it's so dark.", he mused.

"It is.", I told him.

"But, it's only dinner time."

"Yes, but there is that great big cloud, Dylan. It's blocking out the sun. All that ash that keeps falling, that's from the cloud." He looked worriedly at me so I put my fork down. "Thats how you know that it is all going to be okay, the cloud is already falling apart and it will keep breaking and then it will be all gone and it will be sunny again."

"How long will that take?" He queried.

"I don't know Dylan, but I know that it will."

"Mom when is Tamie coming home?"

"Soon I hope." I needed her to come home soon.

"How will she find us though, it's so dark and the streets lights aren't working properly."

"Tamie knows her way home, and we haven't moved, so she'll find her way back and she has her car. She is probably just sorting things out. She has probably tried to call us, but the phones aren't working, darling." He had his heart set on her coming home, but who knew what had happened, but I couldn't think about that. I had to stay strong for my son.

We sat in silence, Dylan looked like he was about to ask another question, so I put some pasta in my mouth, and hoped that he would wait for me to finish eating. I could hear him breathing at the end of the table. I could hear it at night as long as the wind wasn't too loud. I could hear mine. It was getting heavier and harder. I could feel my lungs being coated and irritated by the ash.

I dropped my fork and it clattered to the floor, hitting my chair on the way and splashing sauce on dirty floor. I knew I had to clear it up later, and that that would move more ash back into the air which would set my asthma off. I started crying and I couldn't stop, even though I knew that Dylan could see me; I might be the only person left alive to be there for him. For all I knew she could be dead.

I heard the chair scrape dully on the carpet and then the soft pad as he slid to the floor. He went into the kitchen and got some kitchen roll to wipe of the mess I'd made. He was careful not to move much of the ash, but a little tickled my throat. I breathed slowly as I could to try saving another dose.

"Mom, are you okay?" He asked lifting my face with his warm hand.

"Yes, I will be when your sister gets back and I know you're going to be fine."

"I have you Mom, but I can't wait for Tamie to get home."

She needed to get back soon, or I needed to find more medication. Once I ran out it was only a matter of time until Dylan would be on his own, he was too young to deal with it.

I shook off the thought, and picked up the dishes, scraped my left overs into a tub. I hoped it would be okay the next day. I boiled the kettle for a little hot water and washed the dishes carefully. Dylan dried. I looked in the fridge again, and then the freezer and tried to plan what we would eat for the next few days.

Tamie,   6:05 p.m.

As I ran into the parking lot all I could see

was the large number of angry people smashing cars and jumping from the roof of one car to the roof of another. I crossed my fingers and prayed that they had somehow overlooked my car. As I breathed deeply, heading to the back of the lot. I tried to avoid the psychotic mob as much as possible. That's when I saw it: my car. It was in shambles. Every window was broken, the hood was crumpled inward, and one of the headlights had somehow been entirely removed. When I got close enough to really assess all of the damage, I realized the worst part yet. They had taken one of my tires. This wouldn't be a problem for some people, accept that I had never learned to change a tire, and at this point there was really no time to repair this car enough to get it to Texas. As I turned back towards the school in despair, a police car screeched its way into the parking lot from the street. The officer got out of his still running car and pointed a taser at the nearest offending person.

As he was shouting warnings and commands

at the violent men and women, a stone flew from somewhere behind him and hit him squarely in the back of the head. He ducked, and he put a hand to the spot where he was hit. I could just barely see from where I was that blood had started to spread through his hair. He fell to his knees and his face hit the ground with a sickening thud. If it had been any other day besides May 31st, 2032, I would likely have helped the injured officer. I would have called him an ambulance, and I would have even had some harsh words for whoever had thrown that stone, but today I needed a car.

So instead of helping the poor man like I could have, should have, I ran over to his still running car and got ready to drive it away. The only thing that stopped me was that, as I closed the door to this nice, sturdy police cruiser, I noticed the pistol still attached to the officer's hip. After a moment of thought I decided that the gun would likely be safer in my hands than in the hands of one of the lunatics that were still busy smashing the other cars to pieces. I went to his unconscious body, and I took the police officer's gun.

Once I had my hands on the weapon the crazy people in the vicinity converged on the officer and began to beat him like they had beaten the cars. It was bloody and very violent, but it was also not my problem. I needed to get home.

The door to the cruiser shut with a thud, and I pressed my foot pedals. The car was much faster than I had anticipated, so I tried to keep it slow. As I made my way through the winding streets away from campus I glanced in the backseat where I had thrown my bag full of food. There, just under the back seat was where I saw the shotgun. This wasn't the type of cruiser that they apparently kept criminals in, because I didn't imagine that they would put someone bad in the back seat with a gun just underneath them and no separation between them and the driver.

But, then again, had I not just committed a felony and became a criminal? I had just stolen a police cruiser and left a man, maybe to die, in the middle of a parking lot full of crazy people.

No, I couldn't think that way. I had only done what I needed to do, and with the world in chaos that was all I could afford to think about. I needed to get home, and I would do whatever I needed to in order to see my mother and little brother again.

Continuing to drive, I pushed the buttons on the police radio. The constant stream of panicked calls from other officers was too much for me to listen to.

"They've taken over the university, " shouted one.

"We need backup in dorms, " cried another.

And some woman seemed to be talking in code, "255 to 673 that's a 989, " she would rattle off again and again. I pushed one button after another until the radio finally went silent.

Just as I got the broadcasts to stop I looked out through the windshield and saw a park overrun by a mob of college students. There was one lone man near the outside of the park attempting to gain what little control he could over the situation. He was clearly in police officer's clothing, and when he turned towards the road I was on, I could see the fear in his eyes. He knew he had no control. He saw the police car I was in and began to wave to me for help, but as our eyes met, he clearly recognized what I was and resigned himself to running from the mob.

I finally make it onto the interstate just as the cloud begins to overtake the university. There was nothing I could do for anyone left in the city. All I could do was continue to drive, and hope for the best. I checked the gas gauge and thanked the heavens that the needle was hovering over the "F." I would have some time before I needed to stop again. Sadly, the cloud would overtake me long before then. After only a few minutes of driving, I had to slow down, because the cloud surrounded me in near total, grey, darkness.

7:45 p.m.

The gas pedal was more sensitive than I was used to and maintaining a comfortable speed was difficult, even with the mostly barren highway. People were too busy rioting and looting, but it wouldn't be long until they started trying to run. The darkest clouds were visible in my rear-view, meaning everyone who could would try to head south. No one would outrun it, not even me.

Mom and Dylan would have a day at least before the weather got too bad, but I could have been wrong. What did I know about sciencey stuff like that, I'm a sociologist. I only knew about people, and knew that the ash in the air wouldn't be good for mom's asthma. She wouldn't last long, and after she is gone how long would Dylan last?

I remembered when he was born. It was during one of those times where dad wasn't too bad, I think he didn't want to risk a miscarriage of the little boy he always wanted. He was so small, he liked that I was ginger, probably because I was the only ginger in the house. He always pulled my hair, but I didn't mind. He was so sweet. I remember being so terrified he would end up being as big a bastard as our dad.

I had some relief that he wouldn't end up like dad when the cops finally arrested him and a restraining order was issued. He didn't have visitation rights even, he couldn't influence Dylan. The genes were still there, he could still end up like that.

I started to play with him a lot. Colouring, or at that time scribbling, with him. Playing with his dinky cars, and blocks. Spelling his name with the colourful squares, just so he could push them over and giggle at the mess. When he was old enough to walk, I played ball and hide and seek with him.

With mom working a lot and unable to keep up with his energy, thanks to the asthma. I spent most of the time with Dylan. I picked him up from daycare, fed him dinner, gave him his bath, gave him another bath after I finished my homework, and another before reading to him. Mom usually came home to tuck him in, but I was still there.

When Lily moved in next door, she would come over and help take care of Dylan. I wondered how she was, whether she was trying to get back to her grandma. Maybe her grandma would be helping mom and Dylan.

I realized I was crying, and that my heart was pounding. I quickly wiped my eyes on my arm and took a few breath. "Talk to yourself. The mind responds better when your verbalize. Stay calm. Focus. Crying is a waste of water, and won't help me get home any faster. Just drive. Stay alive, stay focused."

Book 2

2 Days After

Tamie

My mind was blank, focused entirely on driving, until the sign for the next rest stop came into view. A its gas station symbol marked on the sign. I checked the needle marking gas, and it settled on empty. The car had enough to get me to the gas station, or at least I hoped it did.

The car managed to get to the pump, but I doubted it would bring me much further. The gas station was empty, with no vehicle or life in sight, though it was still in reasonable shape. I eyed the pumps and it occurred to me, they had likely been emptied when all of this started. Even if there was any gasoline left in the tanks, they probably wouldn't work.

After several deep breaths of the remaining filtered air, I put on my mask and stepped out of the car. There might have been some things I can scrounge to help me with my trek. I brought the knife and pistol with me, fumbling briefly to find the gun's safety.

As I approached the building I could hear muffled voices inside the station, but no one was visible from the windows. I circled the building, gun trembling in my hand. Behind the building was a pickup truck, its back filled with food, water, and blankets. Nobody was in sight, .

I didn't have any food, and very little water, and might have been able to syphon the gas. I had done it it in my freshman year of high school, and it turned out that I could still have managed it. doing so could have killed the people in the gas station, but they might have tried to kill me if they found me. I took a closer look at the supplies in the truck, and the assortment of canned food made it all the more tempting after having been eating dry pasta and cold soup.

I went to the station's back door and put my ear to it. The voices within became clearer, and I was able to distinguish the voice of a man and a woman.

"We can't stay here, " the man said.

"Why the hell not?" The woman's voice was sharp, reminding me of an old woman in a sitcom.

"Because someone will eventually poke their nose around a gas station for supplies."

"Then we'll scare them off."

"An empty gun will only scare people for so long."

"Then what do you suggest we do?"

"Rest here a bit longer, but then we keep going. We'll look for supplies along the way."

I pulled away from the door as quietly as possible. I needed those supplies. Dylan and Mom would need them, too.

As quickly and quietly as I could I took out boxes of food, and cases of water from the back of the truck and put them in my car's trunk and backseat. I left the blankets behind, I didn't need extra blankets in the heat. Along the way I found a cut hose that reeked of gasoline and an empty gas canister, they had been syphoning gasoline. I pushed those aside and took what supplies I could get, including a crowbar sitting with half-a-dozen cans of fruit. In the end less than half their supplies were still there when I had finished moving them.

I carried their syphoning tools and carefully, inserted the hose into their gas tank. I hoped I was using the right end of the hose, I started to suck with the gas canister ready. My heart pounded while I waited for the gas to come up, terrified that the pair would see me. Soon the horrible tasting brown liquid came up and I put the hose in the tank, resisting my body's desire to cough by spitting. When the canister gas stopped flowing I hurried back to my own vehicle, and poured the just over half-full container into my own car's tank. I put the hose and canister in the trunk when I finished.

Then I heard the back door into the station open and I rushed into the front seat of the car, the man crying out angrily. I slammed the door and started the car, thanking the universe that this wasn't a movie cliche where it didn't start. I hit the gas, the car accelerating quickly onto the entrance ramp. I briefly scraped the side of the car off the barrier in my rush. I could see the outline of the man in my rearview right before I got onto the highway. It felt like hours until I slowed down, my heart racing.

3 Days After

(A transcript collected from the BBC archive.)

You are listening to the BBC news on the world service. The time now is..... [static]

Our top story today is the ash cloud from the supervolcano eruptions of Sumara Tabo and New Zealand's Taupo, with the largest eruption at Yellowstone.

New Zealand has been completely covered by the ash could with warning that Australia and.[static]

[static]....No further reports have come in from Sumatra, only that China, Japan and eastern Russia will be under ash cover in[static]

[staic]

The yellowstone eruption continues to cause increasing levels of disruption across America. Unfortunately we cannot cross over live to our reporter in the US as we have lost connection with the other side of the Atlantic. However, we received the following report from our correspondent in the US earlier today, and to the best of our knowledge the following account is accurate.

[static]

"Following the eruption of the supervolcano, under Yellowstone National Park, the ash cloud has now spread to cover most of the United States. Many cities across the nation have been obscured in darkness, with Chicago, Omaha, Kansas City, Des Moines, Minneapolis, Denver, Oklahoma City,

Albuquerque have all been smothered by a substantial layer of dark grey volcanic ash.

We are getting reports from local broadcasters further away from Yellowstone that there are lower levels of ash build up. Where areas have experienced rain many citizens are experiencing building collapses caused by ash build up placing too much weight on the roofs. Its thought that as little as a metre of ash in combination with moderate rainfall could cause such events to happen.

Visibility is poor, with eyesight being restricted to approximately 3 meters in areas near to volcanic epicenters, whilst further away broadcasters are reporting visibility is slightly better further away...

Of course one of the effects of these eruptions will be a severe food shortage around world. Whilst the initial period of ash settling could boost crop growth, on this scale it is likely to suffocate any plant life that it covers.

The authorities around the world have released a number of announcements warning people to remain inside their residencies, and that if they must travel to make sure that they have a map of the area in which they plan to travel through, as the majority of satellite navigation systems have become unreliable. "

That was our reporter in the field, People across the world are expressing shock at events that are unfolding. Sally McGowan has been out talking to some of them....

4 Days After

Mrs.Gallie and Dylan

Being able to see the bare wall at the back of the cupboard is something that I've seen very few times. The majority of these times had been when moving house, or leaving a holiday rental cottage, but, last night was the straw that broke the camel's back.A tuna pasta bake where the pasta was substituted with stale bread was particularly difficult to eat, although Dylan seemed not to be too phased by the latest travesty to leave the kitchen.

We could not make it any longer, so I called Dylan down from his bedroom, and told him that he needed to get ready to come to the shops with me. I reassured him that he would be fine, as long as he stuck by my side, which seemed to fill him with enthusiasm for our little trip. I wished that I could have taken in some of his excitement, but my mind was heavy with the worries for the future. This could be the last time I leave the house, my supply of asthma medication was quickly going down. Even with the old inhalers that I found at the back of the medicine cabinet, and in old hand bags, I still didn't think that these would get me to the other side.

I'm couldn't be sure how long I'd been contemplating the situation that I have found myself in, but Dylan appeared to be dressed and ready to explore the outside world. Before we could leave though I told him we needed to look in the winter box, where we kept all of our winter clothes during the summer months. My scarf was already in my coat pocket, but I needed to find him something, to stop him breathing in the ash. There were lots of single gloves, and an old woolen scarf that moths had ravaged over the years. Eventually I came across an old dressing-up bandana from a western fancy dress costume. I checked to make sure that I could tie it around Dylan's face. Thankfully it was just big enough.

Dylan was now really excited, especially by the Bandana covering his mouth. Before we could go out I told him to go and find me his swimming goggles. He scurried up the stairs towards his bedroom, from which I heard a great deal of noise as his toys were spilled over the floor, in the search for his swimming goggles.

As he came down the stairs, I pulled out my scarf and wrapped it around my mouth.

Dylan put on his swimming goggles.

"I look like a space cowboy", he declared giggling.

"You certainly do", I spoke warmly, "now you must remember to always put these on while this ash cloud remains overhead, okay?".

I picked up my rucksack which I placed by the side of the door from my last walk, and looked back at Dylan. He nodded, his cheeks poking up over his bandana as he grinned.

Wrapped up, we ventured out of the house and into the grey storm of ash. I was worried that I might be faced with one of my asthma attacks again as the wind hit me opening the door, it gave me and Dylan quite the shock, causing me to lose my breath momentarily. Fortunately I managed to calm myself, I took Dylans hand and we went out into the street.

We walked, shuffling through the ash and along, what I assumed to be the sidewalk.

"Now Dylan", my voice was muffled by my scarf and the wind, but he turned to look at he, and nodded to show that he was listening.

"When walking through the ash you must walk

slowly, it's hard to tell what's under foot and where the curve of the sidewalk is".

He nodded agreeing, slowed his pace and moved closer to my side, already having slipped his left foot onto the road several times now.

Half way down the street I quickly realised that walking all the way to the shops would be too much for me, never mind Dylan. I had misjudged the force of the wind and could not put Dylan through it on his first ash walk'.

I directed Dylan towards one of the houses at the end of the street, and up to the door.

"I thought we were going to the shops?", wondered Dylan, his voice smudged by the bandana.

I walked Dylan to the front of the house, the door was locked, but most people in this neighbourhood didn't lock their backdoors. So Dylan and I went around to the back of the house, but the door was locked, perhaps the family that lived here locked up the house and fled hoping to return.

My theories were being proven wrong, as Dylan pointed out an open window. I helped him up through the window and I quickly followed.

The room we entered was a living room and covered in ash, from where it had burst in through the window. We went into the next room, the kitchen and removed are scarves and bandanas.

"Are they not in?" wondered Dylan brushing the ash from his goggles.

"I don't think so"

"I thought we were going shopping?" Dylan repeated his question.

"The weather is a lot worse than Mommy had predicted, so we won't go all the way into the shops today." Dylan looked at me puzzled, concerned of whose house we had plainly broken into. "I don't think the people who live here, will mind if we take some food Dylan, we can always host a party for them when they return to make up for it if you like".

"They won't mind?", Dylan confirmed.

"Not at all, now let's have a look around shall we?"

Dylan agreed and looked through the cupboards at his height, and I had a look in the cupboards and shelves above the kitchen worktops.

Dylan found a variety of fruit. "I found some bananas here", he called. I reflected upon how long it had been and knew that the fruit would be rotting by now, if not already rotten.

I knelt down by Dylan and looked at the apples and bananas and oranges, upon their surface they looked alright, but having picked them up I saw that they were covered in mould.

"If you ever see this white fluff on food Dylan, this is mould, you shouldn't eat food with mould on it or it'll make you sick", I placed the fruit back and picked up some canned peaches, Dylan's favorite fruit. He watched me as I went to pick up the can, "But if its in a tin can that means the food will stay fresh", He nodded understanding and smiled looking up at the peaches, "yummy", he declared, "If it's in a can", I added.

We packed up the tinned peaches and various other tinned and dried foods that we could find.

And left through the way we came, upon Dylan's request, who did not want to disturb the house too much for when the family returned home.

"Don't forget your bandana", I reminded Dylan. He brought the bandana over his mouth but couldn't remember how to tie it. I showed him, untied it and watched him do it himself.

"Good job", I smiled.

The winds of the ash cloud were just as strong as when we had left, it was certainly a good job that we did not journey all the way to the shops.

We walked back into the house and brushed off the ash from our clothes onto the welcome mat, Dylan giggled, "You have stuff in you hair".

"So do you", I laughed rubbing his hair, shaking the ash onto the ground, from his blonde mop-like hair.

We took off our coats and trainers and walked into the kitchen, I pulled out a bowl and spoon, poured the tinned peaches into a bowl for Dylan, who went into the dining room to eat them as I packed away the rest of the food.

5 Days After

Lily

Annabelle and Maria stayed stayed in the car. Marcus and I walked along the streets searching for people, and an explanation, but they proved hard to find. The odd people we saw, ignored us. Marcus grabbed a guy not much older than ourselves, and asked him for help.

103

"Don't we all." That was it. He just walked off in the other direction, looking back and scowling at us. It was unsettling.

"Marcus, let's just go back to the car." I grabbed his arm and pulled on it.

He shook me away. "Fine"

"So?" chimed Annabelle as slid back into the car

"Looks like we're lost."

"What do you mean Marcus?" Maria spoke slowly and carefully next to him.

"What do you think I mean Maria? We're lost and I suppose we've just got to keep driving." The atmosphere was so tense I felt as if the pressure was going to crush me.

We seem to drive in circle through the city and there is no one to ask for help or direction.

Marcus's driving made me feeling sea sick as he is snakeded his way through abandoned cars. Chaos had erupted in the aftermath of the ash cloud, and everyone panicked, with no one taking charge, the situation had only been magnified.

Having paused we tried to figure out a navigable route through an abandoned traffic jam. Cars pulled over the the edge of the road and some just left where they had come nose to tail with another. Driving on the sidewalk was possible, but there was chaos there too, bins knocked over, abandoned bikes.

Someone tried to open the door to the driver's seat. Marcus put his foot on the accelerator and narrowly avoided a small car half up on the sidewalk. I looked behind us, and saw a man stumbling and stamping, shouting in our direction.

Marcus didn't stop once we were far enough away, he just kept driving until we had no real sense of where we were anymore. I certainly didn't know this part of town. We saw the odd person and where he could Marcus avoided them, taking the next street away from them. If he couldn't he just sped up till we were away from them.

"Marcus, stop just stop." Maria was beginning to panic

"No, we have to get out of here."

"We've gone this way and that way and we are still in the city."

He turned to face me. "I'm tyring."

"Marcus." I shouted. There was a boy crossing the road oblivious to us heading down it, Marcus wasn't paying attention and as he looked at me he must have put his foot on the accelerator. The boy didn't see us coming until we were only feet from him. Marcus turned and hit the breaks, and we all flung forwards. I saw the boys startled face before he disappeared, knocked from his feet and landing in front of us a small distance away.

They get out of the car to check if the boy is injured. He is conscious however, cannot walk properly anymore.

"Marcus you killed him." Maria shouted. Marcus, his white knuckles continued to grip the wheel .He didn't respond to her.

I jumped out the car and ran to the boy. He was holding his leg crying. He looked about seven yet no parent or adult came running over to make sure he was alright. I brushed the hair out of his eyes; it was a little wild, all brown and curly. The breeze hindered my efforts.

"Where's your Mom and Dad?"

"I lost them" He grimaced with pain, when he moved to look at me.

I looked around and back to him; there didn't seem to be anyone around. He watched at me with brown doe eyes. The others still hadn't come over.

"You lost them?"

"I can't find them." He murmured, as he choked back tears.

His parents could be dead, and leaving him would be classed as abandoning, but his parents could also be alive, which would mean taking him with us could be seen as an abduction.

"Do you want to come with us?"

Marie walked over as I asked him, "He is not coming with us Lily."

"We can't leave him. He has no family, and now he can't walk." I kept my temper.

At this particular moment, Lily starts to doubt her friends and becomes disappointed about the way they reacted in such a difficult situation.

"Can you walk?"

The boy tried to stand up and fell forward as I caught him.

"That's a no then." I spoke to no one in particular. "I'll carry you".

Annabelle's door was already open so I urged her to move over.

"Who's this? We can't afford to pick up strays." Marcus grumbled.

I was shocked by Marcus. This was a boy not a stray cat or dog. He should have shown more sympathy, taking into account the fact that he had hit the boy with his car.

"Marcus we're helping him"

"Correction: you're helping him. He's your responsibility!" I didn't appreciate his tone but he was my only ticket to safety and I wasn't going to tear that apart. I mumbled something about Marcus' behaviour; if he happened to have heard me he continued to ignore me.

I sat the boy on the edge of the seat and he

dragged himself in, having to lean on Annabelle's lap. I slid in so that his feet rested on my lap. One was beginning to swell.

"What's your name?" I asked.

"Johnny"

"Hi Johnny, I'm Lily."

No one else introduced themselves. I didn't introduce them either.

As Marcus continued to drive we all slept sardonically. Johnny held my hand as he fell asleep.

I turned to look out of the window. The sun was setting, the ash making the usual warm glow a metallic grey horizon, and as the silverlight faded the world we knew, descending into darkness.

I couldn't really calm myself down to get to sleep. I dwelled on the events that unfolded a couple of hours ago. My friends had been prepared to leave a injured boy alone in the chaos of the city; particularly bearing in mind that it was due to us that he was injured. It was difficult to comprehend their issue; had I really endangered the group through my actions?

6 Days After

Mrs.Gallie and Dylan

Dylan peered out his window at the neighbor's house. He remembered that it had been Lily's house before she went off to school. Lily was Tamie's best friend and she came over to spend time with Tamie often. Dylan remembered that she was very nice, and he hoped that she was safe.

Looking at her house now, Dylan saw that the windows were cracked and the siding of the house was dented in some places. The small quakes that had been happening for the last few days had not been kind to this building, I was thankful that Dylan didn't seem to pay them much attention, and in all truth nor did I until I heard the creaks of our neighbours house. It did not look anything like he remembered it had before, or even how I remembered it for that matter.

On this particular day, the wind blew dust and ash into the spaces in the broken windows. Dylan could just barely see the dust beginning to pile up on the edges of every window. The window closest to him looked into Lily's kitchen. He could see the glow from where someone had left the refrigerator door open. Dylan imagined it was probably quite cool in there by now, and if there was any food left in the fridge, it had spoiled.

Dylan turned away from the window and returned to playing with his blocks. With a sudden boom, and a deafening crash, the kitchen he had just been watching so intently exploded. Dylan rushed back to the window as I ran to him to see if he was okay. The fridge in the neighbor's house must have ignited the dust and ash and caused an explosion.

From the window, the small glow of the fridge had now turned into a raging inferno. Every bit of dried dust that had accumulated in the abandoned building had caught on fire. The wood floors and the frame of the house would also catch quickly if someone didn't put it out soon. I knew no one would. I thought about the possibility of our house being caught up in the inferno as well, but our lots were far enough apart that I wasn't worried. Dylan and I sat together and watched silently.

It took a few hours for the fire to burn itself out, and by the time it was over there was nothing really left. Some of the roof had fallen into the backyard and sat there smoldering for a while after the rest of the fire died out. We both sat there, Dylan in my lap mesmerized by the dancing ash outside which didn't seem to be affected by this large new addition, instead, the glow of embers from the house mixed with the dark grey ash falling from the sky and looked a bit like snow.

Radio Broadcast

This station has interrupted its regular broadcast programme at the request of the United States Federal Government. for the foreseeable future the this station will remain on air to broadcast News and official information for areas assigned to them.

The following message has been verified.

The authorities would like to remind citizens that sanitised water levels are at an all time low.

They would like to ask citizens to conserve as much water as is possible. The authorities are working in tandem with the military to try and provide a sanitized source of water for the majority of the population. Further updates on this situation will be available on this station in the coming days.

This concludes our broadcast. Please stay tuned for further announcements.

This station has ....

7 Days After

Mrs.Gallie and Dylan

Me and Mommy walked out of the house hand in hand, and down the street just as we had done before. Only this time the ash was much more violent, my bandana and goggles were missing and Mom had also lost her scarf. The winds were so strong that the ash appeared to fly up from the ground just as heavily as it rained down upon it. The houses that lined the streets coughed, unable to breathe, others screeched as the ash covered their glazed eyes.

The cross roads at the end of the street had vanished and the row of houses seemed to stretch on forever, into the horizon and into the depths of the ash cloud.

We stood in the middle of the road, the ash almost up to my knees; and then she let go of my hand and drifted down into the ash.

She walked at a slow melancholic pace through the ash like a boat through water, within a matter of moments I had lost her, I tried to run after her but she remained a shadow in the distance. It was as if people were grabbing my legs under the ash preventing me from running to her.

"Come on Dylan", she paused at a house and called out to me; "Keep up Darling" and then she walked into the house.

I ran into the house following Mom, but couldn't find her, searching from room to room, amongst

furniture covered in ash. Photos holding what remains of families and fine art work were covered
in ash, ruined by the fall of civilisation.

As I re-entered the entry I saw Tamie standing
half way up the stairs, her hair, fiery red like a
lion's mane seemed to have a life of its own, it
waved around in the air growing before my eyes.
Her mouth struggled to open, as if her lips were
unable to break apart,

"Dylan! Sweetie! I'm always here for you!"
she cried with her lips finally snapping.

And then she jumped upon me, holding me
down and preventing me from moving. I looked
down the staircase, to see my school mates Matthew,
and Thomas slowly crawl towards me, they were
weeping, as the tears ran down their cheeks burning their skin.

"Look your friends are her to come and play
with you Sweetie", Tamie hissed, still holding me
down on the staircase.

"Let me go! You're not Tamie!" I screamed.

And then they vanished.

"Tamie!" I cried out. "Where's the real Tamie?"

"Dylan, over here Dylan", it was Mom, she was staring right at me from the end of the street.

I immediately ran after her and then paused, her skin was falling from her cheeks, her eyes stared blankly at me. Timidly I stepped towards her and then the ash began to surround her, her skin was torn away by the ash until she was nothing but a skeleton.

Mom held me tightly; I woke up screaming and crying in her arms.

"It's ok, it's ok", she comforted, "It was just a bad dream pumpkin, just a bad dream", she continued to reassure me, rocking me in her arms.

"Shhh..." she spoke softly, her warm hold was comforting.

Tears still ran down my eyes as I breathed heavily, "The ash killed you", I blurted out grasped in fear.

"I'm still here Dylan, I'll always be here", she continued to rock me in her arms.

"We're a team, we'll get through this together;

all the way, you'll see". We sat there in my bed for a while as she comforted me, and I think I may have done the same for her.

I broke the silence.

"When will Tamie be back?" I asked, unable to get the other Tamie out of my mind.

"She was probably held up someplace, you know Tamie, she's probably helping someone out some place". We sat in silence, her rocking soon made me sleepy again and she began to recite a poem which sent me to sleep.

8 Days After

The Ward Family

The Wards were involved in all kinds of activities around their house. Chris was snoozing on the couch. Lola was playing with one of her dolls, imagining a better life for herself. Millie lay on her front in her bedroom, trying to study, believing she'd be back in school soon.

Mr. and Mrs. Ward were in the kitchen talking about their own affairs, away from the disaster they were embedded in.

They then heard a knock on the front door. The family's first thoughts were that it was the police asking them to evacuate, or some neighbours looking for help.

Mr. Ward opened the door to find a slightly dishevelled looking man who could have been about 65, with grey, messy, wet hair, pale eyes and a brown baseball cap over his head. The poor man was wearing a black raincoat, stained with ash.

Lola ran to the door and peeped from behind Mr. Ward's legs. The older man noticed her. "Oh, I didn't realise you had children with you, " he said sadly. "I didn't mean to bother or steal." The Wards were surprised by the man's words.

"You must have been walking through the ashes for a while", commented Mrs. Ward. "Are you okay? What is like out there?"

"I'm alright, " the man replied, "I have a handkerchief to help me breathe out here. The whole area is coated in this damned ash. From what I heard a volcano erupted up north. I never expected such a nice place like this to go so mad."

"Anyway, sorry to bother you, hope you'll be alright", he groaned, and walked out into the ash fall and disappeared. "Wait, " shouted Mr. Ward after his shock had subsided, but the man was gone. "Wow, he must have had somewhere to be, " said Mrs. Ward.

Mrs. Gallie and Dylan

It really is surprising how quickly the cupboard becomes bare, although I suppose that this is because they haven't really been full for quite some time. It's only been a few days since we last left the house for supplies.

I let Dylan have the last of the proper bits of cereal from the packet, the rest like everything else is just dust. After trying to revive some stale bread in the toaster, I settle for the fact that the paste I can make out of the leftover cereal and a little bit of water will have to do. I spotted Dylan trying to eat some of the toast that I had pushed to the side, in favour of the paste. He pulled a disgusted face, before I'd just taken a picture of it, which successfully summed up the problem that we faced. I asked him what he thought we should do today. I expected him to respond with something fun, like building a fortress. But to my shock he's the one to suggest that "We should go shopping", to replace what we had either eaten or could no longer use. I could feel my eyes start to tear up, and so as not to distress Dylan any more than the breakfast already had I turn my back to him and looked out the window, as if all I'm doing is checking that the weather might let leave to scavenge. It looks clear enough, and whilst I know the weather outside can change in an instant, I decided that he is right, and that we did indeed need to leave the house to get some more provisions.

Turning back to look at Dylan, I say that if that's what we're going to do, that we need to do it sooner rather than later. I tell him that we should go and get ready right that moment, and that we'd do the washing up when we'd returned.

Can you remember what you wore last time we went out?', he nodded, Well go an put similar clothes on'.

He pushed his chair away from the table, and I followed him out of the room and up the stairs. When alone in my room I found a scrap of paper which I had made the night before. On it were three lists, for things that we could not do without this trip, things that would have been useful to have; and finally items that I knew deep down were gold-dust requests and that probably no longer existed. Looking at the lists I realised that the last list was becoming progressively shorter. Not because I'd been able to find them, but because I'd started to realise that they were no longer of any importance. They had stopped being necessary to daily life.

Soon Dylan was knocking at the door asking me whether I was ready to go. I found myself so lost in my own thoughts that I had to look down to remember that I still need to get changed. I called out to remind him that he'd be needing his swimming goggles, rather than hearing him respond I heard the sound of a little footprint scurrying off to find swimming goggles. By the time he returned I'd successfully changed, so we headed for the front door.

We walked out into the cloud, rucksack on my back and Dylan in hand. The cloud was more of a light flurry to day, our visibility was reasonable and the winds were much softer than previous walks. I decided that today we would make our way to the local row of shops, about half an hours walk away, put probably more of an hours walk now that we were trekking through layers of ash.

The shops were about the halfway mark to Dylan's school, so we both knew the route we'll, but this didn't stop us from losing our bearing several times, unable to distinguish the uniform rows of grey houses with the next.

We walked into a small general store, which we had often used to pick up bits and pieces for various dinners and domestic supplies. I wondered if we would ever return to that society, but quickly moved my mind onto more pressing matters.

The shop was unlocked just as the other shops appeared to be down the street, but many of them were of little value to us in this present climate. There were three other shops, including a newsagents whose door was open and now the building had been defeated by the ash. A florists, in which all the flowers had undoubtedly shriveled and died, though you couldn't actually tell with the windows covered in ash. And a hairdressers, who Dylan always despised, as he didn't like to have his hair cut.

From what I had taught him from our previous expedition I asked Dylan to find the food for us as I waited at the counter. On the counter was a selection of books, under the small cardboard banner Mr. O'Donalds Book Recommendations'. Dylan quickly came back with two boxes of eggs and a bottle of water.

I looked at him warmly, not wanting to remove his giddy smile over his treasures but knowing that I had to. He understood, comparing the eggs to the apples he had found before, and went back to search the shelves.

One of the books was titled Home Gardening by Samantha O'Donald', the book included a pack of pea seeds, curious as to whether I might be able to find the various other components needed for home growing this could be an interesting activity for Dylan, and would certainly teach him about plants as well as getting him some fresh food.

I placed the book into the bottom of my rucksack as Dylan approached.

9 Days After

Local Radio Broadcast

(A transcript taken from the emergency broadcast system.)

This Station has interrupted its regular broadcast programme at the request of the United States federal government. For the foreseeable future this station will remain on air to broadcast news

and official information for areas assigned to them.

The following message has been received and verified for your local area:

The local authorities would like to remind you he residents that it is in your best interest to avoid leaving your homes, and going out into the ash cloud.

Rest assured that the local authorities are doing everything that they can to resolve the situation.

This concludes our broadcast. Please stay tuned for further announcement.

This station has been [static]

10 Days After

The Ward Family

The air was thick with the ash and dust that hung and drifted. It coated the ground and the car. It covered the roof of the sheds so that the shingles were no longer visible. The piles were too heavy to be moved by the hot, slow breeze even off the fragile leaves of the plants and the withering vegetables.

The ash came in every time anyone opened the door. It seeped in through the vents above the windows that had been left open so it didn't get too muggy and stuffy in the house. It clung to the shoes that had been worn on the day the storm hit. Clothes had been washed, even jackets and scarves since then, now that water was short they had to be brushed down in the coat cupboard, but it still clung to them.

There were footprints going to the living room, to the hall, to the stairs, to the office, to the kitchen, to the door and back again with shoes and bare feet. There were even small prints of snow boots from when Chris thought it was just funny coloured snow that covered the ground in summer.

He went through stages of thinking that it was all fun and games, a little bit like Christmas because Daddy was home all the time, at other moments he was bored and nightmare-ish, running up and down and round and round, screaming because he wasn't allowed out, and he hadn't been to the park in days. He was bored of playing with his cars on his own. Hungry hippo's could only entertain him for so long. When the girls were younger they had lost some of the pieces of the big puzzle, and there were only so many time his mother could keep him entertained by playing hide and seek before he once again asked if he could go outside.

"You can't go outside darling, " His mother crouched down to pick up the cards from where he had been playing on the floor.

"Why not?" He looked at her straightening up from his bent over, cross legged position.

"The ash, it's bad for you."

"Why?" He whined.

His mother snapped, "Because it is. Why don't you go play with your cars or your planes?"

"I don't have a plane." He stuck his bottom lip out.

"Pretend." Millie rolled over on the sofa, "Stand up and stick your arms out Chris, " and he did.

"See, now you're a plane."

He started running. "Mom, Mom, look at me I'm a plane."

She simply rolled her eyes. "Go and show your Dad."

He ran towards his Dad's office and fell with a thud and began to cry. His mother and sister rushed out into the hallway.

Chris had tripped on the rug, and was lying exactly where he had fallen, arms still stretched out like a plane, crying.

Millie grabbed his hand and pulled him awkwardly to his feet, and their mom wiped his tears. "Do you hurt anywhere?"

"My knee." He managed to pronounce through gulping sobs.

"What's all this racket out here?" The door of the office opened.

"Chris fell over, Dad." Millie said.

"Well what did you do that for, silly?" His dad ruffled his hair.

"I was a plane, Dad." Chris stopped crying a

little and smiled.

"Ah. Well it looks like you crashed. Maybe we need some more lessons, yeah?"

"Rich, he's cut his knee. What if the dust gets into it?"

Looking up from his son to his wife he seemed calm. "We can wash it out honey, it will be fine. Put a band-aid on it and we'll keep an eye out."

"What if it gets infected? We can't get to the doctor's. What do we have in the basement?"

"I'll go and look for a band-aid and disinfect it now, and do it before you send him to bed. He'll be fine. You're a tough one Chris. You're a plane. Planes are tough." At his son's smile, Mr Ward went downstairs to check the basement. He went to the chest of draws where he had put the medical supplies. They had enough for a while, provided that no one got seriously ill, but like everything else they seemed to need medical supplies had been one of the first things people looted. He hoped that the cut wouldn't get infected. It was unlikely, he tried to convince himself. Liv was just worrying too much.

Lily

"How are you going to look after this kid.'
Marcus started to rant at me but I'd already made
up my mind, this kid needs my help, and it would
be wrong of me to leave him behind.

Anibell and Maria were just behind him, and
from their stances I could tell that they've all
agreed on what they think is the best course of
action. I focused my attention on Marcus, waiting for the moment when his eyes would show me
that he's exhausted all his prepared speech and
was starting to ad-lib.

"Look it's bad out there, I don't think that
it's a good idea to try and move anywhere right

at this moment. I'll halve my rations with the kid for the time being and see if I can't get him feeling a bit better. Anyway you're the one who hit him with the car."

I saw Marcus shift on his feet, after he opened and closed his mouth a couple of times before Annabelle stepped forward, giving Marcus a scornful look as she usually does so. "The thing is Lily, we've all got places that we'd rather be, and well, the kid is just going to slow us down, isn't he?"

I'm taken back, I thought I had found a common friendship with these people, and that, like me, they would be more than willing to help somebody in need. "So you're giving me an ultimatum?"

"Yeah, I guess we are." Maria pipes up.

I'd never thought that my friends would put me through this type of ordeal. We'd hurt this kid. We should really all have taken part in looking after him.

"Well, if that's how you feel, ok then. You all seem to have made up your minds, so I doubt that there is much I can say to change anything."

"I guess that is settled that then." Marcus'
voice was hoarse.

I nodded, trying to fight back tears.

It only took them a matter of seconds to disappear into the ash cloud, but I could hear the
cars engine for a few minutes afterward..

I walked over to where I sat Johnny down, and
despite his ordeal he gave me a little smile. It
didn't make up for losing my friends though, but
it certainly took some of edge off.

I looked up at the road ahead of us, and whilst
I couldn't see very far ahead, the sky definitely
looked darker than it did when we left the University.

"Wait here Johnny. I'll see if I can find something to help me move you off the road. Then
we'll figure out what we're going to do next."

Johnny nods.

After a couple of minutes scavenging I managed to find a broken packing palate that I combined with a scarf I had in my bag to make a

makeshift splint. On my way back to the kid my mind went back to Tamie. Would she have left me as the other did? Everything might be alright if only I could just find her.

After I had secured Johnny's leg as best I could, I got us moving. When Johnny asked me where we're going, all I had in mind was "somewhere safe."

11 Days After

Mrs.Gallie and Dylan

I woke up around 4:00am, my throat was chalky and I was unable to breath. Recollecting an asthma attack is not an easy task, nor is it something I often find myself doing. I can not recall much. Merely the frustration of being unable to control myself and the fear that any one of my nexts desperates gasps would be my last.

When I finally came around I felt as if I had been punched in the lungs, I found myself leaning off the side of my bed still gasping for air, but finally my lungs were beginning to appreciate it.

In my panic I must have woken Dylan. As I pushed myself up back into bed and saw him standing at the door; flashlight and teddy in hand, ready for action.

Either my yelping breaths or the bang as I fell off the side of the bed must have woke him, but I chose not to inquire.

"Hey there son, sorry did I wake you?"

Dylan nodded and then joined me under the covers.

"Me and Sebastian wanted to know if you we're all right", he asked sleepy-eyed. Dylan placed his flashlight onto the bedside table next to a novel that I had been reading a couple of weeks ago, but had never returned to.

"That's very kind of you", I said still trying to claim a steady breathing rhythm, "And Sebastian" I added placing the battered teddy in between the two of us.

"But Mummy is fine", I continued.

I turned to the my side reaching for the inhaler I kept under the bed, to help me back into rhythm. I attempted to disguise this act by brushing my hair, but even sleepy Dylan detected that something was wrong.

"Has the weather made you sick Mommy?"

I turned to him placing the inhaler under the covers. I gave a shallow grin, "Sometimes Mommy..." explaining anything to a child can be a difficult task. I held the inhaler under the covers and took a deep breath. "Sometimes Mommy needs this". I raised the blue inhaler and handed it to Dylan. "It's called an inhaler and it helps Mommy to breath". Dylan nodded slowly understanding what I had told him, or at least appreciating the seriousness of the object. "Only the stuff that's inside it is running out".

"We'll have to find you some more", Dylan smiled and raised his sidekick Sebastian.

"I'm sure you will", I picked up the inhaler back from Dylan and used it. The inhaler was empty.

"See what I mean?", Dylan nodded, but his expression was that of uncertainty.

I rose from the bed leaving Dylan with Sebastian in my room and walked to the bathroom.

I pulled the cord turning on the bathroom light, looking into my blood shocked eyes, and my vain attempts to brush my hair. Next to the bath a small cupboard contained contained various shampoos and our first aid kit and hidden towards the back my inhalers. There was one left at the back hidden under some unravelled bandages which we had used the better half of for a Halloween costume.

I took the remaining inhaler form the cupboard and quickly placed it into the pocket of my pyjama bottoms, knowing that it would be better saved for a more serious attack, if I could not find more medicine within the next few days.

But now was not the time to worry about the

fact that almost every place I'd searched for an inhaler so far had been empty. Tomorrow that would have to be my top priority but right now my son was concerned for me, so I went back to the bedroom to rejoin him.

As I re-entered my room he was sitting up, cross-legged, with Sebastian on his lap.

"Come on now lets go back to sleep now, I'm still tired and I sure Sebastian is", I moved around to my side of the bed watching my son as he tracked me around the room and then went back under the sheets.

"Would you like to sleep in my bed tonight?"

He replied with a hug, "Yes please".

"Would Sebastian like to join us?"

Dylan raised his teddy and nodded its head in reply.

"Then you can join us to", I smiled and then lay back down onto the pillow.

Dylan stretched across to my bedside table and turned off his flashlight.

Lily

The child was starting to wheeze, cough, and sob a little. I heard the sound of wood creaking a little.

"Hey?" I looked over my shoulder at him, "Does it hurt?".

"Yeah."

"Okay, down let me see what I can do." I sat him on a rock and I noticed that the wound on his thigh seemed to be getting darker and look infected. I looked at him, he seemed so small and so scared. "Hey, soldier, come on smile, that's a cool battle wound it looks like you fought with a pirate with a sword." I start to adjust his splint.

He smiled and seemed to brighten with that

"Johnny, huh? You know there was a pirate named Johnny, John Silver actually, he was quite the pirate he was so smart that Blackbeard and Captain Flint were scared of him."

He's eyes mooned with shock. "Really? No one ever scares Blackbeard."

"Really, he was so scary, and you know he hurt his leg too, that made him even stronger."

He frowned at his leg as I finished adjusting the makeshift splint. "Do you know any priate songs?"

He shook his head,

"I know one it's an old shanty called Randy Dandy" I picked him up, and began teaching him the song.

I started to notice light and noise up ahead. There looked to be trucks moving around. On one of the trucks that came close I read "UNIT 268". It looked like a military base.

"Hold on tight Captain J." I ran as fast as I could towards the the trucks and shouted to them

I could see some of the people were civilians, they getting water and food.

A tall dark man was on top of a truck was

shouting at the crowd "Move! Keep moving! Stop pushing!". The crowd was shouting and pushing to grab the bottles and packets that were being distributed.

I noticed a man on foot pushing people along and I approached him, "Hey! I need your help this kid-"

"We're at full capacity ma'am" he continued to move people along.

I jogged after him, "Listen, he's hurt. His leg may be infected."

"We're at full capacity, " he said, "we can't take any more. There's another outpost further along."

I put Johnny down and told him to sit and wait for me, the base was loud, soldiers shouted, generators and tanks rumbled.

I pulled my shirt above my mouth and nose to avoid inhaling the dust that was being disturbed. "Listen, let us in please, I'm healthy and strong enough to help you."

He continued to walk away, "I'm in engineering. I'm good with electronics."

That seemed to get his attention, "Dale, garb the kid get him to medical. You follow me."

I followed him past the rowdy crowd and past the medical tent. Everything seemed so bleak and so dark. This wasn't the big apocalypse they said in revelations, it was a progression to several smaller ones. Someone did say that the world won't end with a bang, but a small painful whimper.

I was brought out of my thoughts by a large man, a cross between the Hulk and a monster trunk.

"I was told you know your way around the electricals. We're headed to the power plant to try and revive it. Think you can help?"

"Sure, just tell me what to do, and I'm your girl."

He patted my back with large hand and lead me to meet the rest of the team.

At the plant I learnt that his name is Lt. Drammeh, but everyone called him Lt.Crack, apparently he had a knack for cracking peoples heads open.

Like so many others after the ash cloud descended the plant was dark, it turned out that silt from the air had blocked the vents and clogged the hydrosystem. Lt.Crack got two of his strongest to clear the silt as fast as they could.

"The backup needs fuel. The tank got creaked and what it leaked out." A small blonde man said.

The lieutenant ordered a man to bring tools to fix the leakage.

The blond man said from around another door, "The transformer seems to have taken on some damage. We'll need that to be repaired to get this running."

That was my cue.

"Yo, chica, it working yet?" Apparently militarily didn't bother to remember anyones names.

I rolled my eyes. "Not yet, no."

Robin, the resident Don Juan, showed me how to fix the filter and transformer system.

I went through the steps required to fix the filter and transformer system, but nothing happen. I tried the steps again, then I heard a low hum of the plant coming back online.

"YES! We're back on lieutenant . See chica, I told you we can do it." The team highfived and cheered at their achievement. This meant they could properly stored medication and food, it meant that Johnny had a chance.

The lieutenant stood and his voice boomed, "Alright boys there's a storm coming let's head back to base before we're buried in this shit hole."

As we left the plant it started to thunder and the wind howled around us, the group started to run towards the trucks.

"Hurry!" I heard one of them shout, the first group got into truck and drove towards the base.

The bag I was carrying broke open with the supplies falling out them. As I stopped to pick them up, I heard a soldier screaming my name from the truck.

I saw them begin to drive off, so I sprinted after them. It looked like I wasn't going to make it, the truck seemed to slow and I saw the back door open. Robin and the small blonde soldier stood there with a cloths wrapped around their faces .

I ran as fast as I could and jumped into their arms they pulled me into the truck.

"You know chica, you're all sorts of crazy." The group of soldiers laughed as we all headed to base.

12 Days After

(A transcript collected from the BBC archive)

You are listening to the BBC news on the World Service, the time now is 6:00.

As the ash cloud spread across the face of the planet the rest of the world starts to feel the adverse effects of the natural disaster that has paralysed the world. Much of our communication has been affected due to technical failures so we can only bring you the following facts.

Much of the US is engulfed in a large cloud of ash, which was caused by the eruption of a supervolcano in the Yellowstone National Park on the 31st of May 2032[static]

The spread of sulphur-dioxide particles has been worsened due to the opening of jets streams at the North Atlantic ocean. The effect of such jet streams have been to fast track the ash clouds movement throughout the globe.

Scientists have today warned that the Europe should prepare themselves for an extended period of cold weather as they predict one of the main consequences of this eruption will be a substantial cooling of global temperature by approximately 5 degrees centigrade.

Whilst snow and ice are uncommon for this part of the year, a government spokesperson today advised motorist to take care when traveling as both could occur. A group of independent scientists have warned that rivers in some parts of the world may even freeze over, which could lead to further power shortages as hydroelectricity dams cease to work.

It is now feared that Europe will eventually face the same level of severe food crisis as the US, New Zealand and Indonesia. With a large amount of crops being wiped out by much cooler temperatures.

The next news broadcast will be at..... [static]

13 Days After

Mrs. Gallie and Dylan

Ash had built up outside the front door, and I considered closing it. I was going to have to do something to clear the path out to the street, or at least the little bit that was near the house, otherwise the ash would to start to get into the house, and that would only make my asthma worse. As

much as this needed to be done my first priority; however, was to find asthma medication. Although my chest felt better, I was still a little bit
shaken so I decided we would stay close to the
house. I knew some of our neighbours had been
asthmatic, the 2029 New Years party had made
that clear, and many of them had left town.

Breaking into the neighbor's house wasn't nec-
essarily a difficult. I had watched enough of those
crime drama shows on TV. I would have rather to
avoid it, but necessities had to change.

Before we had left the house, I'd gotten Dylan to find an old tea towel whilst I found a large
roll of duct-tape left over from Christmas present
wrapping. I secured the tea towel to the window
pane placing the duct-tape in parallel to the sash
and gave the window a short sharp blow with my
fist. Rather than breaking the glass it just re-
pelled my hand back towards my body. I looked
down at my smarting hand, television made this
seem a lot easier. As I looked around the front
garden for something heavy to use in place of my

hands, I caught Dylan's face. He looked as though he was in shock, and I quickly moved to comfort him with a hug: "What's the matter?"

"It's bad to break into houses."

I'd always been so careful to try and instil within him the ideas of good and bad, managing, primarily by luck, to avoid much of the grey area. To Dylan breaking into a house was in the black, but that was before the ash.

"Normally." I hesitated. "But we're in a very special situation now aren't we."

Dylan looked puzzled.

The ash has changed things, so that means that we have to change the way that we act to reflect the world that we live in'.

So sometimes things are okay and sometimes they are not.' Dylan mumbled to himself, then slightly louder: How do we know?'

I'm really sorry I can't tell you, I'm not totally sure myself'

He nodded. "We need food?" He asked, looking up at me hopeful for confirmation. I nodded back to him unsure whether it was society or me that had changed. I turned back to Dylan who was sifting through the ash to searching for something to break the window with.

Dylan pointed out a rock to me, which I lifted and successfully smashed the window I used the towel as a mat over the broken glass so that Dylan hurt himself when I helped him in.

We walked through the house on tender hooks. I remembered the nice young couple Jules and Catherine Smith, the ones who had held the party at New Year's here. Jules was asthmatic but Catherine often had his inhaler: he would have forgotten it otherwise.

I went upstairs to search through their medicine cabinet, which I assumed to be in their bathroom, though eventually located in a draw in their bedroom. Dylan had remained downstairs rummaging through cupboards I guessed from the clanging of cans hitting a hard surface which echoed up the stairs.

I rummaged through the draw and managed

to locate a few things that would help ease my pains and one inhaler towards the back of the draw which I quickly slipped into my pocket. The couple must have taken the majority of their pharmaceuticals with them when they left, or at least that what I hoped for their sake.

Dylan and I spent the rest of the day moving from house to house. It was hard not to look at the family portraits on the walls; families brightly lit standing on the beach, dusty wedding pictures, laughing grandchildren behind proud grandparents. Mrs. Sommerville's house was full of wilting flowers and dust covered oil paintings, all her own. Mr. and Mrs. Proud' with their triplets, pulling faces in practically all of their photographs, except for one, which was at their christening. I almost felt sorry for the vicar. Even Mr. Wickets house which was scattered with pictures of his drooling great dame were touching to look at. Dylan and I used to tell silly stories about him before the clouds, and now him and his dog were gone.

Around the other houses we found some other

various supplies, but not quite the quite the amount I had imagined. Dylan was just pleased that he had managed to find some biscuits, and various canned fruits, including his loved peaches.

On our way home, Dylan wondered where we were, as I looked around the ash.

"I must admit son, I'm not so certain myself", I replied cautiously.

Dylan tugged my arm. "I think it's this way." I placed my trust in him, following down the street and we eventually met a cross road

"Well done", I congratulated him. His smiled above his bandana.

No more than half way down to the house I suddenly stopped, as my breathing became frantic, I wanted to remove my scarf and breathe the air, but in doing so I knew that I would also be breathing in the ash. I pushed forward, Dylan recognising the seriousness of the situation and held me steady to the front door. Entering the house we both dashed in, my lungs felt as if they were collapsing in upon themselves.

I removed my scarf flinging it to the floor and using Jules' inhaler. I breathed a sigh as my breathing slowly became less frantic. Dylan looked up at me in relief and hugged my ash coated jeans.

14 Days After

Lily

After the storm, for a few days the sky went from a dark blackish colour to a lighter grey colour. The military had been in and out protecting structures and supplies around the base. I watched as they brought in the injured to get treated, some of them didn't make it. It smelt of death and chemicals.The air felt like it held you by the throat.

"Come on, let's go get food." Johnny was pulling me by my shirt to follow him out.

Dale, the medic had done a great job on his leg, Johnny wouldn't stop running around despite his injury still healing and was talking to everyone. He was, oddly, a little ball of light in that bleak, dreary environment.

I got up and took his hand, "Okay. Captain let's see what they are giving us today."

The survivors gathered around the large truck where food was being distributed. Johnny and i included.

One really scruffy man shouted out suddenly. "What the fuck is this?" He held up the packet of food for the soldier to see.

"Move, others are trying to get their share." The soldier I first met told him.

"You call this a share, this less than last time. How the fuck is this supposed to last us two days?" the scruffy man retorted.

"There are more people and not enough food,

" the soldier said, "everyone's rations are cut down."

This aggravated the crowd and they began to shout in protest.

A woman from the crowd ran to the truck and tried to grab more food, one of the soldier picked her up and violently threw her out of the truck. The crowd exploded and began fighting the ground troops to get to the truck.

It became an all out riot, blood was spilt and I could hear bone crunching. Screams and howls of pain pierced through the rumble of machines.

I saw a soldier I knew, Robin, and the Lieutenant run towards the crowd with their weapons in hand.

"Move back!" Lt. Crack's voice boomed, he grabbed two men from the crowd and knocked their heads together, the move that earned him his name.

The soldiers atop the truck, started to fire their guns into the air. "THIS IS A WARNING, MOVE BACK NOW!" This just infuriated the crowd and made them more violent.

I was pushed into the riot, and Johnny's hand slipped out of mine.

"Lilly!" I heard his panicked voice call out to me, I saw him being carried away by a soldier, and I pushed and shoved my way through the sea of insanity to get to him.

"I'm coming Johnny." I called out to him, he looked so scared.

His eyes were wide and watering. I had to get him to safety.

I grabbed his hand and tried to pull him away, the soldier didn't even budge. He pushed me back and continued to walk.

I hit the soldier in the head and tried to take Johnny from him. He turned back and I noticed that it was Dale.

"Give him back." I yelled.

"Listen, I'll get him to safety. The truck there is going to carry him and the rest to a safe zone. Come with us and I promise I'll get you both there." Dale looked at me to get my answer. Gun fire erupted of to side, I was pushed and pulled as people tried to either escape or to fight the military.

I lost Dale and Johnny. Though I briefly was able to glimpse them getting into the truck.

I tried my best to shove through the crowd to get to him, the military had become aggressive and were shooting at the crowd. Physically fighting with them, it was becoming chaos.

I saw the truck's doors close. Johnny kept calling out to me, as I tried to get to him. The crowd got worse and the violence escalated to unbelievable levels. It felt like the stories Ama would tell me as a kid about the demons of Hell.

The truck drove away. Johnny would be safe. Dale likes him and will take care of him. I had to worry about myself. I had to get out of the base.

15 Days After

The Ward Family

The alarm went off at 6:00, as it had every weekday morning for the last 8 years. As normal, Mr. Ward grumbled, turned it off, and tried to go back to sleep, but he failed. He grimaced; when he had nothing to do he couldn't get back to sleep, but when he had to be in the office at 8:00 he could blindly turn off the alarm, and have to rush to get ready after his wife's 6:45 alarm, and avoid dipping his tie in the children's cereal as he kissed them goodbye.

Reluctantly he rolled over and got up, pulling on his robe and slipping into his house shoes. Trudging downstairs quietly, he went to his office. He used it for informal meetings or to do work. There were a few of accounts that needed going through, an article about a french economist's new theory, and a fax from a business requesting a loan so as to expand its market beyond North America.

Mr Ward picked up the fax and started pacing while he read. He considered the proposal on the paper. The business had many viable options and expansion had been the next step for the company when they sent the fax, but for all he knew there may not have been a Europe, or South America, or Asia or Oceania to expand into. He threw the pages at the wall. Dollars and cents were a brilliant career; that's what he had been told. Go into money and you'll get money; money makes the world go round. If he had been a doctor like his mother wanted him to be or farmer like his great grandad had been then at least he could be useful. He could help out. He could be productive. He could have continued, but he was a banker.

There was a brightly coloured plastic truck hiding behind the desk. Chris liked to go into his Dad's office simply because he wasn't supposed to, but he wasn't very good at being secretive. He usually forgot something, or left a sticky hand print on the desk, or he would just go bright red when Mr. Ward came in and end up telling everyone. His sisters found it hilarious.

Usually Mr. Ward found it funny. It was cute, and he didn't really cause damage, but after being stuck in the house with him going a little wild and the two girls bickering relentlessly, it was not amusing. He kicked the truck towards the door, but it was heavier than he had expected, and his slippers offered little protection. He cursed.

He hobbled over to the desk chair, spinning it around to face the window. He saw the vague outline of his wife's car, a grey shape outside the front of the house. He had parked his around the back; he hadn't thought about moving her car. He found her keys in the kitchen. He probably ought to move it, he thought, all the disaster films show people brutally murdered for their cars. At least if it was behind the house it couldn't be seen from the main road, and if someone attacked the house then they could run to the cars and escape. Moving the car would be doing something useful.

He changed upstairs, waking his wife. He shoved on boots by the door, wrapped a scarf around his mouth and nose, and left, a little flurry of ash entering as he opened the door. He adjusted the seat and turned the key. It made a whining noise and went quiet. He tried again and the car shuddered, but still refused to start. According to the gauge, the car was full of fuel, and his wife had driven it when the ash had started coming down.

He popped the the hood, because it seemed

like the appropriate thing to do, but when he looked at the engine but it was all metal and plastic to him. He always just took the car to the mechanic when it broke, gave the guy the money, and didn't ask any questions.

He grabbed a bucket from the tool shed and a piece of old hose he found. He did at the very least know how to siphon off the fuel. His Grandad had taught him one summer when they were clearing the farm. He sucked on the tube, and put the end in the bucket. He spat violently, cursing. As the fuel trickled slowly into the bucket. He kept spitting, attempting to get the gasoline taste out of his mouth but only replacing it with the dry, suffocating taste of ash. It coated his boots and collected on shoulders and in his hair.

Eventually the flow of gas stopped completely, and by then there was a fair amount in the bucket. He lugged the bucket to the shed, and tried to pour it into a rusty jerry can. He curse when he spilt some onto the floor and splashed his shoes. He couldn't even pour fuel into a can.

Mrs. Gallie and Dylan

I sat in bed, up early from the sound of ash
of brushing against the window, luckily it didn't
wake Dylan. It gave me a chance to figure out
how long the inhalers should last me. Based on
how quickly I had been going through them, as
long as the ash didn't get any stronger that I'd
be able to cope for at least a couple of weeks.
There was a super-store on the edge of the nearby
industrial park, and I could only pray that just
from the size people had not already picked the
store completely clean. It was about 6:30 when
I decided that I had to get Dylan up and ready
to go. I'd normally let him sleep, but there was
a break in the ash cloud so we had to take our
chance while the weather lasted. he was a little

dazed by the early hour, however, after I'd told him that we were leaving the house, he was full of excitement and ready to go.

Leaving the house at 7:00, the weather had changed considerably, and I had to re-evaluate the plans to head to the big store. Instead we headed down the road towards the better of section of the estate on the other side of the park. Crossing the flat park was a relatively quick process, as the ash had settled to resemble thick snow. It gave me an opportunity to tell Dylan that we need to try and collect as much food today as we can. I explained that if we could get us much as we could carry, maybe we could stay at home for a few days. He agreed, and after a short spell of silence as we looked around the park, spotting the children's play park which looked more of a death trap than normal, I broke the silence.

What would you like for tea tonight?'

Dylan looked up at me, and adjusted his hat, as he could not get to his head to scratch it. After a few moments he said he declared that he'd either like Mac N' Cheese with hot dogs, or some beans on toasts, because he's not had either of these in a while. Although I'd got a stash of inhalers, something about the ash still made me feel a little uneasy, and I decided that I should give another lesson.

"Okay well what do you need to make beans on toast?"

As quick as a flash Dylan responded with beans and toast, as if the question was designed to insult his intelligence. It was another one of those moments that at any other time might have been quite cute, but in the harsh grey of the ash-covered park it felt tainted with the bittersweet nature of the situation. That tactic having been defeated, I decide to change my tact.

Where would you find beans?', Dylan responds within a tin', but before I can tell him to be serious, he picked up on my irritation and added in a cupboard'.

"What do you need for toast?". I'm expecting an answer along the lines of a toaster, but Dylan instead answered with a serious answer of bread, and as an afterthought he added he wasn't so sure where he would find this. I looked up and see that we are nearing the edge of the park, and pointed to the first big house I can see.

I'll show you in there.'

Radio Broadcast

The ash cloud over the United States was very dense in many states and visibility was still poor.

The thick cloud of ash made it hard to make a phone call, difficult to send an email message via phone or computer, and tricky to film a video message to a loved one.

Some satellites in High Earth Orbit couldn't

send or receive data at all, with it near impossible for signals to penetrate the dark veil hanging over America.

NASA from Florida and the ESA from their base in French Guiana tried to improve connections with their various satellites, so that citizens will have the ability to contact each other.

The engineers at the space agencies were successful, but the satellites in Low Earth Orbit wouldn't work either.

Regardless, in Wyoming, Colorado and Nebraska, most to all forms of communication had gone down. They were shut off from the outside. From each other.

16 Days After

Mrs.Gallie and Dylan

Dylan was in the dining room down stairs drawing one of the spacemen from the book he had been given to read in school.

I was in my bedroom, trying to disguise my struggling breathes. This was a particularly violent asthma attack, my breaths were frantic and

I was losing control of my arm and leg muscles. I attempted a series of breathing exercises to little avail.

I had to resort to one of the few puffs left in my inhaler which quickly helped me to steady my breathing.

I looked up to see Dylan standing in the doorway, looking at me holding his little bear Sebastian.

"Hello darling", I greeted him, straightening my back reclaiming my breath.

"Are you okay Mommy?"

"I'm fine Dylan, I'm...", I paused missing a breath.

Dylan came up to me and gave me a hug, he held onto my legs tightly.

"Mommy's good darling." I smiled down to Dylan who looked up at me with puddle like eyes. "I'm grand." I kissed him upon his forehead, "Now come on, let's go and have a look at those drawings".

17 Days After

The Ward Family

Millie leant against her closed door. Once again her parents were arguing over something silly, and she could still hear Chris wailing downstairs. Lola was throwing a ball at the wall. It was worse when it rained, because their dad was stuck in the house. He couldn't go and try to find food,

185

not that he often came back with anything. He couldn't even go to the tool shed. No one else was really allowed out, not her or Lola or Chris, and their mother didn't want to leave if the air was going to be difficult to breath.

Lola either calmed down enough to stop or lost her ball. The rain started making odd, squiggling patterns in the dust on the window as each drop raced towards the ground to create a sludge on the window sill. Occasionally the sludge would drip down. She saw it fall from the gutter, and she assumed it would be dripping from each window down to the next until it finally pooled in a dirty puddle on the ground outside. The ash created little piles in the garden. The gutter, however, had begun to get clogged with the wet sludge.

The rain did seem to clear the air a little, not much, but when she wandered over to the window Millie could see the ground, and she could make out the vague shapes of the shed and her dad's car, but it certainly wasn't the flat distance she was used to. She picked up her violin and leant against the wall in the window alcove. She started to play quietly.

It felt normal to play; it meant it could just be a dust storm, and that it would pass. It would mean that Dad would go back to work soon, and she would go back to school, and so would Lola, and Chris wouldn't have so much bottled up energy, because he would go to the park with Mom. Millie walked to the door while she was playing, paused, and opened it. Everyone used to like it when she played.

19 Days After

```
Lily
```

It became a warzone outside and it didn't look like it's going to get any better. I saw an empty tent, and I decided to hide out there until the situation is under control, ducking and weaving till I got there, and decided to hide behind one of the jeeps.

I heard someone enter the tent, and held my breath.

"Tell the rest of the men to protect the ammunition the last thing we want if for these animals to get their hands on it." It was Robin's voice. "Chuck and I will drive up to the other base and call for help, tell the one's who can to get to the other base."

He continued to relay orders to the other men, I stayed hidden, not fully trusting them anymore. "Yes Sir.", I heard the foot soldier's head outside and the trucks being loaded.

Robin came out of the tent and headed for the jeep I had been hiding behind, briefly stopping to look over the chaos.

I quickly climbed into the back seat while Robin was distracted and remained hidden until we had left the base. I didn't want them to realise that he had a stowaway.

Shifting my position to try and avoid shock, it didn't help. The jeep swerved, I was knocked about. The jeep stopped and I found a gun being pointed at my head.

"Jesucristo en un palo." Robin shouted, "What the hell are you doing here, kid?"

"Woah, I'm not gonna do anything. Please put that down."

He put away the gun and glared at me through the review. "Talk."

"I just needed to get out of there. Are we headed to the same base as Johnny?"

"Yeah, we're going to wait there for help. God know's if any one will come." He looked at me., "Strap in chica it a bit of a drive."

I turned and looked outside, it was actually like we've been transported to the second layer of hell.

I surprisingly slept throughout most of the ride, exhausted from everything that happened. Robin made a couple of jokes about how I'd have a line of men if I ever went to Cuba. I dreamt of Johnny, of Grandma and of Tamie. The line between dreams and memories began to blur.

The car slowed and jerked to a stop, "Yo chica,

get up, we here now." Robin smiled at me as he got out. He and Chuck, the other military personnel, began to unload the truck.

"Your boy is inside that tent." He pointed out where I needed to go.

Jesus, this place was in even worse shape. The earlier storm must have wash down some mud, because everything was covered with it. It smelt like the autopsy room I had been in to see my parents. Not exactly like death but cold and musty and kind of stale.

There were more soldiers here but less weapons from what I could see, most of it looked like communications equipment. I spotted Lt.Crack off to the corner speaking with another man, the man looked to be his superior and not happy.

I walked past a group of adult women that looked scared and annoyed. One lady stood of farther off chain smoking, her fingers were shaking and she had a bandage around her arm.

The tent just overflowed with people, most of them women, most of the wounded. I looked around for Johnny hoping to find him uninjured, stepping over bodies.

"LILY!" I whipped my head to the direction of the screeching, and saw him run towards me with his arms opened. He began limping as he leg still needed rest.

"Come here little man." I picked him up, hugging him tight. I saw Dale walk towards me.

"Hey." I saw him shift around uncomfortably, "Listen, about leaving yo-"

"Hey listen, no worries. Thanks for keeping Johnny safe." he nodded and took Johnny off my hands.

Johnny showed his own conquered corner, we sat there talking and catching up. I looked up to see Robin walk in and signal Dale. They talked in heatedly but hushed tones. It looked like Robin had something really terrible to say, Dale looked upset and started to show his hands round. Dale then shoved Robin to the side and told him to "Respectfully, fuck off."

He then gathered the medics that were assisting him to tell them what is going on. I moved a little closer to hear what is going on.

"They lost the armoury to the rioters. Some of our men are dead. There's a group that's on their way here, they want food and supplies. They want us to take the healthy ones and leave the rest here, no food no water."

That's all I could bear to hear, they wouldn't leave Johnny here would they. Oh God, that place wasn't safe anymore.

I needed to find a way out, they're probably a couple of hours away.

I sat outside of the tent, observing the area. Just then gunfire could be heard far off. I saw soldiers running around everywhere. Two other jeeps approached the base with crazed civilians driving it. It was the rioters.

Robin ran past me with a gun towards the formation aimed at the cars.

A voice pierces the air. "Did you think that you could hide from us?"

Everyone grew restless. "Did'yah!? Well fucking hell. Food, water, medicine. Did'yah think you could keep it to yourself." The voice drawled out.

They came in bursting violently, gunfire was ever. Everyone ducked and ran away, it was just like at the the other site, chaos.

I ducked back into the tent and grabbed Johnny. I carried him out towards the far side of the base so he wouldn't get hurt.

We hid behind a food truck. They aren't stupid they won't hit what they're after.

I saw the soldiers get into formation and prepare for an all out war. Innocents were getting killed. Some of the rioters went into the tent and began shooting at people. I could see a medic running towards the screams of the injured.

He then suddenly fell, a rioter shot him from behind. I shut my eyes and hugged Johnny closer, muffling him so we wouldn't get caught.

Dale suddenly loomed over me. "Give him to me. I'll make sure that he get to the safe zone." I told Johnny to go with Dale and that he'll keep him safe.

Suddenly, he fell over me and Johnny. We were sprayed with bullets, I look over and I see blood. Dale got up and clutched his arm.

"Oh my God, you're bleeding!" I screamed in a hoarse and panicked voice. He looked at his shoulder and winced, "It's alright it's not too deep and they can fix it later." We grab Johnny and Dale takes the lead.

"I have to get him to safety. I promise I'll look after him you find yourself somewhere safe and lay low." Dale takes Johnny's hand.

I nodded and ran as far as I could away from the bullets. I saw a large backpack beside a tent, it was filled with provisions.

I grab it and I saw Lt. Crack's tent had been ripped open, I jogged to it to see if he was there. It was empty, a set of keys sat on his makeshift desk. The jeeps. I remembered that they are bulletproof. I grab the keys and headed for the green one with the red stripe. I drove away as fast as I could from the area.

I hoped Johnny was going to be okay. I continued to drive hoping it was in the right direction.Just driving away, as far away from the madness as quickly as I could. I just wanted to go home.

20 Days After

The Ward Family

Everyone was in the living room, Mr and Mrs Ward and the two girls played Monopoly in the small light of a single candle. Chris, too young to play the game, rolled his toy racing car through the thin layer of dust instead, making shapes and patterns.

Lola put a hotel of Park Place. Millie landed on it. Lola shrieked with excitement.

She suddenly bagan to cough. At first it was mild, but become a deep hacking and wheezing. She was retching in pain clearly struggling to breathe.

Mr. Ward seemed to freeze unsure how to help. Chris had stopped playing with his car to watch with fearful eyes.

Mrs. Ward ran to the kitchen to get a glass of water. By now Lola was visibly getting red in the face. Mrs. Ward held her daughter's head and helped her to drink. She tried to swallow but choked and spat out the water over the Monopoly board. Mrs. Ward continued trying to get her daughter to drink and breath.

Lola tried to sip again. This time the water went down her throat. The coughing began to recede. After a moment of calm. She clutched her mother's hand. She kept with wheezing breaths and a sore throat.

Her father laid down on the couch by her mother. Her siblings were visibly upset, but rather than worry they pretended it never happened and went back to playing games. Millie grabbed a toy car and tried to join in with Chris.

"I hope that was just a bit of over-excitement and not the ash getting in her lungs, " said Mrs. Ward. "As long as it wasn't anything permanent, " her husband replied.

21 Days After

Mrs.Gallie and Dylan

    I watched Dylan eat his canned fruit and spam breakfast. Only picking at my own.

    "Are we going out again today?" Dylan pipes up through a mouthful of apple.

    "Maybe."

    "Is that a yes or no?" he accused me with the

turn of his head.

"It's a maybe. I haven't decided."

"When will you have decided?"

"After Breakfast. Now, eat your spam" I couldn't help but smile at his persistence.

"It tastes yucky."

"I know. It'll keep you strong for when we you go out", I spoke in a gruff voice pulling a strong man' pose which seemed to amuse him.

"So you decided?"

"Yeah. We're going after breakfast".

When we had finished our breakfast and wiped off our plates we got ready. Before I put on my hat and scarf and helped Dylan with his bandana, and goggles.

"Be a big boy and show me how to tie your bandana for Mommy?" I smiled at him.

He picked up his bandana and successfully tied his bandana with his first attempt. I am indeed a proud mother.

I put on my own gear and checked that my last inhaler was in my pocket. Dylan beamed up at me with his bandana.

I pick up my rucksack. "Let's get going."

Taking hold of Dylan's hand, we headed out into the ash filled air.

My heart pounded, and my rate of breathing increased. A sudden gust of wind hit us. I can still feel the dust attacking my lungs.

We trudged forward, trying to keep my head from directly facing the wind.

My breath building to a chaotic crescendo burst through my scarf catching Dylan's attention. I hesitate to use my inhaler, with only one or two uses left.

Dylan squeezes my hand. "Are you okay?"

"I'm Fine." I glance back, seeing we're barely away from the house. "It feels...so far."

"What do you mean? Mommy?"

It was painful to breath, each gasp sent fire down into my lungs. With each step the lighter my head began to feel. "I can't", I gasped, "Help Mommy back darling we have to go back", Dylan immediately grabbed my arm catching me as my legs gave away.

Dylan climbed under me helping to keep up my torso while we crawled back. I felt my knees scraping against the pavement through my jeans. The pain helped to control my breathing, but not enough. My scarf felt wet after the next cough, and I remember hoping that it was only flem.

I fell through the door, and pulled myself into the hallway so that Dylan could shut it.

He removed my hat but, I couldn't let him touch the wet scarf.

A shot from the inhaler came much to my relief. At first the burning worsened, but quickly settled as my breathing became less strained. Dylan helped me through into the living room and on to the couch in a sitting position. Dread shook me as I lowered my hand from another fit of coughing, a small amount of blood became visible on my palm, I shut my hand hiding it from Dylan. Stale air from our home under siege rushed up my nose down to my lungs and back out through my mouth.

"Mommy. It's okay. You're okay. Tamie will come back, maybe she'll even have medicine for you."

"Maybe", smiling at Dylan's hopeful enthusiasm I clasped my blooded hand, "Yes she probably will" we sat in silence momentarily, "I think we'll stay in today, have a little rest and wait for the weather to break".

I can see his face go dark. "That's okay. We'll go out another day." He got up and ran out to the Kitchen, returning shortly with a bottle of water. "This will help."

"I can't, honey." I brushed back his hair, with me clean hand.

He looked down dismayed, "I just wanted to help."

"I know, and you're doing a wonderful job at being a big boy for Mommy. We just have to be careful of how much we use, especially our water."

His innocent eyes stared up at me, holding the bottled water.

"Leave the bottle here. I'll have a little bit

later. Can you draw me a picture? That'll make me feel better."

His face lit up, he placed the bottle down and ran into the dining room. "I'll draw you the bestest picture ever." he called collecting his box of colouring pencils, determined to complete his task.

Tamie

I was woken up by the sound of loud music with a heavy bass, causing me to forget that I am sitting in a stolen police car in the middle of no-where, outside some random shopping center. A car that was long past the point of being improved. There is just a group of guys that I'm use to having hit on me at the bar, until I threaten that my non-existent six foot two bodybuilder jealousy prone boyfriend would beat on them. But this time, I just ignore them, wanting to rest a bit longer before continuing my journey. No doubt that the group will ignore a parked police car.

The music stops, and the voices of three young men who say "bro" far too often reach me. I watch as I see two figures go into the shopping center, while the other sits on the hood of the car. I watch the silhouette carefully. After a minute or two he starts to come closer until he turns to face my car. He looks around, then walks over to me. I shift my stuff so that my gun is not visible.

He knocks on the car window, and makes a little wave at me. At this distance I can see his features, he is a bit taller than me and far too slim. He wears a woman scarf around his neck, likely a makeshift mask considering the rest of his clothes, a wife beater shirt and baggy jeans.

I pull up my mask and open the car window slightly. "Yes?"

"Was just wondering who our neighbour is.

Was expecting some burly officer, not a cute little redhead." He glances at the supplies in the backseat.

"Well now you know. If you don't mind I'm..."

"How did you end up with a cruiser like this?"

"Cop was hit by some debri, and I needed a fast car."

"Well good choice, uh. We haven't been introduced, I'm Aaran."

I bit my lip, taking a second to think whether he might be useful. "Tamie."

"Cool. It suits you."

The guy took out a runner's water bottle and takes a sip. "Want some?"

My mouth was dry, and I stared at the bottle. "Sure." I rolled down the window and took the bottle.

I took a sip, then suddenly I was on the ground, the door open.

Aaran kicked me in the gut. "Stay there, you fucking cunt or you'll regret it!" He laughs, while pulling the keys out of the car and opening the back door. "Stupid bitch!"

I did not feel the entire body however, I managed to crawl back into the car. I could hear Aaran laughing behind me. "I have your keys, sweetheart. You ain't going anywhere." My hands found the shotgun under the seat, just as he started touching my hips. "Sluts asking for it, guys'll love it."

I flipped over, switching off the safety by luck or instinct. He stepped back as I cocked the shotgun. I pulled the trigger and felt the butt of it jab my side.

His blood splattered the interior of the car, the area around his collarbone was shredded by the pellets. He hit the ground with force. I was out of the car, looking at the dead body. I just froze.

His companions ran out of the store. I turned the shotgun towards them, and fired again.

I aimed at the hazy figures scrambling out of the store. "Fuck off!" I shot again.

One guys ducked. The other grabbed his shoulder. The two were in their car by the time I had cocked the shotgun again. The music started up and I could smell burning rubber as I fired again, hearing metal collide with metal.

My breath was heavy, as the car sped out of sight.

I regained control of my body, and slowly put down the bloody shotgun. I looked at the convulsing body, and crumpled to my knees.

The muscles in my throat constricted painfully, urging something out of my empty stomach. All that came out was bile that burned my throat and tongue. The feeling of the blood was familiar. I remembered when I finally stopped dad, when mom's temple was bleeding. Dylan's nose was bloody. I hit him with mom's cutting block. He spat blood at me when I threatened to hit him again. I did. He didn't test me after that.

Dylan and Mom don't need to be protected from him anymore, but guys like Aaran are still around. I need to protect my family from them.

22 Days After

Mrs.Gallie and Dylan

I sat on my bed taking in deep breaths, fortunately I was not having an attack, but my anxiety of having one outside of the house filled me with such dread that I had decided to hold more regular breathing exercises. Dylan was down stairs, I had asked him to collect my scarf, and his goggles and bandana, ready to venture outside into the ash.

I took one final deep breath and exhaled as Dylan came into the room.

"I've got all the stuff", he announced with a muffled voice, already wearing his bandana and goggles. "Brilliant, thank you very much pumpkin", I took the scarf from him and wrapped it around my mouth as we both ventured downstairs to put on our boots and trainers.

We both put on our coats and Dylan looked up at me, I think he was hoping that I would be ok.

"I'll be fine", I said reassuringly. His cheeks rose around his bandana smiling.

I picked up my rucksack from the bottom of the stair case and we ventured outside.

The ash was particularly heavy, but we knew that we had to brave going into town. Especially if I was to have any chance at finding some more medicine. We walked along the ash filled roads for almost an hour when we finally reached the shops.

I instructed Dylan to have a look for what food he could as I would look for paper towels. However as much as it pains me to lie to Dylan I did not want to have to tell him that I was in dire need of medical supplies, and so I went to the pharmaceuticals, to find anything that might be of help to my situation.

I was looking across the various shelves, pregnancy testers, headache relief, bandages, and then I collapsed. I yelped struggling for air trying to bring myself back on my feet. I felt paralyzed; my arms and legs flailing helplessly without control.

I heard Dylan running through the aisles of the shop closer and closer towards me. "Mom! Mom!" he yelled, calling out to me hoping for a response. I lay their gulping for air desperately unable to reply. His trainers squeaked along the tiled floor as he ran down my aisle.

Dylan dropped down to face me desperately asking if I was alright.

"Mommy, What's the matter? Mommy are

you okay?!"

I struggled to respond but realised and realised that that I should focus on getting my breath back first.

My breaths gradually became slower and slower. As I slowly grasped control of my breathing, Dylan ran off to another part of the shop, most likely trying to find something that might help me.

In a matter of moments my breath had returned to its normal state, but that attack was one of the worst that I've had in a long time, and I certainly didn't need to be confronted by another one.

Dylan came back down the aisle as I was lifting myself up from the tiled floor. He took my arm in assistance, "Thank you Dylan", I said forcing a smile.

He looked up at me with concern and a tear running down his cheek.

"I'll be ok Dylan", I tried to reassure him, but I am sure he saw past my lie.

"Come on now, let's grab that food and leave".

After Dylan had filled our rucksack with a variety of nuts and dried foods, and a few cans of tinned peaches and plums, we left sharing the weight of the bag between us.

The ash was just as heavy as when we walked to the shops, and despite a few hiccups in my breathing pattern we managed to get home in a good time.

Dylan supported me as much as he could as we walked, I was drained of energy, hungry, thirsty and still out of breath.

After brushing the ash from our clothes in the hallway, Dylan helped me up the stairs, "Are you okay, Mommy, " he had asked this several times along the journey home, but I had refused to answer, focused on getting us both back home through the ash storm. "Just a little tired, it's been a long day", I replied with a smile. Dylan walked me into my bedroom and sat me down into the bed.

"Mommy's going to have a little nap now, you go back down stairs and have a bite to eat from the shopping", I rubbed his hair brushing some ash onto the floor of my room.

Dylan gave my a big hug, "Night, night Mommy".

"I love you darling".

The Ward Family

Late one morning, the ash cleared. Convinced a was storm coming in, Mrs. Ward decided to try to salvage as much as possible from the small vegetable patch at the bottom of the garden. She was glad she'd installed it; it would finally come in handy. The whole of the garden was covered in a thick layer of ash, and Mrs. Ward had some trouble finding exactly where the plot had been.

After a couple of seconds of careful probing she was able to find the nearside of the patch from the remnants of some delicate spinach leaves that had been completely destroyed by the ash. She was fairly sure that the strawberries and other things growing on the the surface of the vegetable patch would probably have been destroyed, but that if she could shift the ash off the soil then she might be able to salvage those vegetables that were planted just below the surface, like the potatoes, beets and radishes.

Quickly she started to move the ash with her gloved hands, where she thought that the potatoes should have been located. Eventually she found the leaves and started to pull them up. Fortunately, they looked to be okay. However, at this point she noticed that the air had started to get thick with ash. Mrs Ward then starts to realise that in order to have a chance at saving any of the vegetables she would need help. Knowing that the rest of the family were watching from the windows to lend a hand if she got into trouble, she turned around and beckoned them to join her.

They quickly assembled around her in the garden, and after a few minutes of trying to explain the plan through her scarf, Mrs. Ward decided that it was probably best for her to just show them how the job needed to be done. Soon enough everybody had caught on to what they needed to do, and set about the task of uncovering and pulling out the vegetables. The crops that had been totally covered seemed to be fine, but Mrs. Ward was still wary and promised to be careful with cleaning them off before she would let them be eaten.

Cautious of the quickly changing weather, Mrs. Ward decided that her family had picked as many of the vegetables as it was safe for them to eat. They quickly made their way back to the house. Gathering round the table, they looked at what they had been able to salvage from the ash covered ground.

"I'm quite surprised how big those potatoes have grown. I only planted them a couple of weeks ago, " said Mrs. Ward. Mr. Ward commented that they would certainly make a difference to the

tinned vegetables they had eaten for the past few
meals.

After the rest of the family had left the Kitchen
to get out of their ash covered clothes, Mrs. Ward
turned to look out the window at the garden. The
wind had already picked up, submerging most of
the freshly cleared vegetable patch with a new
layer of ash. Mrs. Ward sighed, "That garden
will never be the same again."

Tamie

I saw other vehicles along the road less and
less often. Occasionally a body showed up, but
I just tried to avoid them. Anything on them
wasn't worth braving the stink of a rotting corpse
in that heat.

"Maybe I should get some gas." I mumbled. "I'll have to scarf down another can of apples to get rid of the taste again." I drummed my fingers against the steering wheel.

A popping sound interrupted my thoughts, and the car started to slow. I checked my gas level, the meter still read a quarter of a tank. I pushed down on the gas pedal and the car briefly accelerated but that was followed by another pop. The car continued to slow, until it was moving slower than walking pace. Then it just stopped, and the sound of the engine dissipated. I tried starting it back up, but the engine didn't even respond.

I grabbed my crowbar, and stepped out of the car. With a closer inspection of the hood I found smoke drifting out from it, barely visible in the ash filled air. I opened the hood, releasing a burst of heat and smoke.

My eyes watered as I examined the engine, wrapping my shirt around my hand so I could nudge parts around. Stepping back I stared at the vehicle. "Why am I bothering? I don't know shit about cars."

My heart pounded, so I swung my crowbar at the engine. "Fuck!" I couldn't help but scream. "I need to get home! You have gas you piece of shit. So why don't you work?"

I took a deep breath. "Nothing I can do. Maybe I can use another car. Take what I can and try every car I see."

I filled my Duffel bag with supplies, leaving behind my cardigan and blouse. Which left me only two tank tops and two jeans. I fitted as much water as I can, and a slight assortment of food as well as the pistol and knife into the stuffed bag. I ate a meal and drank a fair amount before I finally abandoned the car and its contents. I carried my crowbar in my right hand.

Each car I came across I checked, pushing aside stinking corpses in a few. None of them worked, I found beef jerky in one, but they were either missing keys or wouldn't start at all.

Eventually I stopped checking, I decided it was in vain. If they worked, they wouldn't have been abandoned. It was not worth my time doing more than glancing to see if they had supplies as I slowly got through my own.

The Ward Family

Mrs. Ward walked down the stairs into the basement. She needed some cans for the children's lunch, but found Mr. Ward pacing inside.

"We're going to run out of food, " he said. "We got enough from the store before it got too difficult, but we can't go out. The dust isn't clearing. I'm stuck inside this place where none of my skills apply! And all the fuckin' time I have to eat food from just cans."

Mrs. Ward was understanding, "We will stay in our house for as long as possible, but once we have few enough cans that they can all fit into the car, then we'll leave this place. But with the kids at risk of getting sick, I think the best thing for everyone is to stay put."

"That's a good idea", replied Mr. Ward. "I need to go out to find anything that could help us get through this."

"I don't like that idea, " Mrs. Ward said despondently. Mr. Ward was already ready to go, jogging up the stairs to find his car keys.

As he ran outside towards the car, Mrs. Ward followed him, "Honey, we need the fuel."

"I know, but I really do need to go or I'm going to go stir crazy." Mr. Ward uttered. "I love you."

"I love you too, dear.", she responded.

23 Days After

Mrs.Gallie and Dylan

I just lay in bed, vaguely covered by the sheets.
I didn't care what position I lay in each breath
burned. The only position that gave me slight
comfort was being slightly propped up against pillows. Dylan announced his presence to me as he
marched up the stairs. My eyes closed praying

that he might just go to his room and play with his toys for a while. I knew that he'd seen me after an attack before, but I didn't want him to see me like that. It felt different. He slowly opened the door. I heard the slow pad of hesitant footfalls approaching the bed. All he did was pull himself on to the bed and settled down beside me. After a few moments of silence I opened my eyes and Dylan held up a drawing for me to see; the park under a clear blue sky, the three of us enjoying a picnic.

I tried to say that it looked good, but rather than words I brought myself to a coughing fit that forced my body to convulse as pain ripped through it. I fought back the tears, Dylan had seen enough pain and suffering already. It took me a few moments to regain my normal composure; now a drained, painful grimace. My breathing became more laboured.

"Would you like anything from downstairs?" I knew it was Dylan's voice, but somehow it sounded different, he sounded more mature. I shook my head, and felt my chest shift slightly, allowing me to force out a hoarse, but polite refusal. Dylan nodded and then shuffled to the edge of the bed. I closed my eyes and heard the door shut, and I was only vaguely aware of the sounds of his steps going down the stairs.

I don't remember hearing Dylan return, and I feel groggy like I've just woken up for a really deep sleep. For a few moments my lungs no longer hurt, but as if to punish me for thinking that I might have dreamt it the pain surged back spreading quickly from lungs right out to the outer extremities of my body. Dylan handed me a bottle of water, cool from the refrigerator.

He left again, and I could hear him fumbling in cupboards, and the clatter of things falling down.

He brought up crackers, and two jars of peanut butter. I sent him back for a butter knife and some paper plates that we found in a house down the street; the Mackenzies had gone to her mother's out of state when the cloud started coming down. I also asked for more water, with crackers I thought

I might need it. I dragged myself up while he was gone so he didn't have to see. I wheezed when I got myself up.

I spread the peanut butter on the crackers thickly, partially mine, hoping that would protect me from crumbs. He sat cross legged, watching me. I started coughing and he took the knife from me, and started putting the peanut butter on the crackers; he broke one by pressing too hard. He looked slightly dejected,

"Oops.", I pulled a smile, "You can save", I paused again coughing. "You can save that one for me." He smiled placing it onto a plate and going for the next one. That one was more successful.

I stopped him when we had nearly finished the first half of the packet of crackers. There was peanut butter on the sheets, he had it on his face and in his hair.

"That's enough for today. Can you take it downstairs?"

"Okay", he replied licking some of the butter

from the side of his mouth.

He put the plates together and shoved them in the box, along with the crackers and the peanut butter. He tried to brush the crumbs off the bed, but smeared the peanut butter into the sheets.

He trundled downstairs, and by the sound of it threw the box on the side before marching up the stairs again. I heard him open the door to his bedroom and wondered what he had gone to find.

After some banging and moving of toys and boxes, he re-entered my room holding the space-men book he had been given from school. He jumped into the bed and sat next to me trying to find a patch where crumbs didn't scratch his bare feet. Once comfy, he started to read slowly to me, showing me the various vibrant watercolour illustrations of the spacemen as he went along.

24 Days After

(A transcript taken from the emergency Broadcast system.)

This station has interrupted its regular broadcast programme at the request of the United States Federal Government. For the foreseeable future this station will remain on air to broadcast news

and official information for areas assigned to them.

The following message has been received and verified for your local area:

There have been reports of ash particles have reacting with ionised particles in the atmosphere to create electrical storms.

The weather in combination with the ash cloud have combined to create some of the worst electrical storms on record. We have received reports of that heavy rain from such storms has led to the ash becoming viscous sludge. Where the ash has become unstable landslides have occurred sweeping away buildings. There have also been reports of lightning storms causing fires, however, we are are yet to hear of any fatalities from such events.

Residents are reminded to remain indoors whilst the weather is bad, and in no circumstances are they to attempt to any kind of outside repairs to their property until the weather improves.

Citizens who have left their fixed residencies are advised to find suitable shelter as soon as possible and not to leave until the weather improves

This station has.....

Mrs.Gallie and Dylan

Mom was upstairs in bed still. She hadn't left it in a few days, apart from for the bathroom. I had to make tea. There wasn't much in the cupboards; just tins. Mom said she wanted beans, and told me to heat them in the microwave. I put the tin in and turned the dial to two minutes. Nothing happened. I turned it back and it dinged. I tried again and still nothing happened. I tried to turn the light on. It's what Mom and Tamie used to do when the kettle broke or the microwave fuse went. It didn't switch on. I turned it back off.

I went upstairs to tell Mom, Mom has made beans on the stove before, but she had also told me very strictly that I was not allowed to touch the cooker. She was pale and drained, her hair was dirty. Her eyes were bloodshot and her lips were tinged purple. She looked like a person from one of the films Tamie used to switch off quickly when I came downstairs for water late at night.

"I think the electric has gone Mommy." Mom tried to switch on her bedside lamp.

"Oh. Does the stove still work?" She sighed.

"I don't know. You told me not to touch the stove."

"I'll come and show you." She made to move, but it hurt.

"No, tell me."

"I'm coming."

Mom struggled down the stairs. She shouldn't have moved. I could have managed. She stopped at the bottom of the stairs and leant against the wall, breathing loudly. She stumbled slightly towards the kitchen and to the drawer where the matches were .

"Watch me carefully Dylan." She whispered.

She struck a match, but it broke. The second one lit, and then she turned on the dial, sticking the match near it and blue flames appeared like magic. She turned it down so the flames were little. She tried to pull a pan from the cupboard, but struggle to lift out from under the other. She wouldn't let me help. She just slumped against the side and weakly turned off the hob, wheezing.

"We'll have tinned peaches, I know you love them."

Mom moved towards the door, and leaning in the banister, she tried to climb the stairs. I had to help her few times. I tried pushing her up the stairs, but it didn't really helps, she slipped and banged her chin. She stopped for a few minutes, coughing. She took her inhaler, and looked at me worriedly. We then tried again, her leaning on my shoulder, this time it was better, until she fell and I fell too. I bit my lip.

"Come on Mom." I muttered.

"Dylan are you okay?" She sounded tired.

"I'm okay." My lip began to swell.

I helped Mom into bed, moving pillows, and lifting her legs on and covering her up. I ran down stairs and went to get ice, but the freezer had melted. Tamie would have told me to be a big boy. I went to the cupboard and got two cans of peaches, in syrup. They were better than the ones in juice. I grabbed two forks and the can opener and went back to Mom.

She was asleep. She wasn't breathing like normal, it sounded scratchy and painful. She whimpered, a bit like the dog that broke its leg last summer. I climbed onto the other side of the bed as carefully and as quietly as I could. I opened my can, trying not to wake Mom, but it made a horrid noise. She just moved slightly.

I tried not to get too much syrup on the bed, but it dripped down my chin and stung my lip. I had already got peanut butter on the duvet the other day. They were big peach slices. I left my tin on the dresser, and put Mom's, with the tin opener and a fork next to her bed so that she could eat it when she woke up. The stairs must have exhausted her. I went to play in my room.

Lily

I didn't think I'd be able to escape but I did. I didn't know the direction that I was heading or where I was going. With my hands on the wheel and my eyes on the road oblivious to the landscape, just focused on driving. Since the beginning of this nightmare there hadn't been a plan, just the desire to go home, back to normality or whatever shred of normality was left. I couldn't think methodically. I was following my instincts. Letting them lead the way.

A farm house came into focus. I knew I needed

somewhere to stay over night. I hadn't slept nor stopped since the beginning of this terror.

I forced these thoughts to the back of my mind as I parked the car in the barn next to the house.

Hoping the house was either empty or its residents would at least let me sleep in the barn, I knocked on the door and waited patiently. No answer. I knocked again. No answer. I thought, "Maybe no ones home."

The front door of the house was unlocked, so I entered.

No lights in the house were on but some light still came in from outside.

The dining room table lay beyond an archway, and a large crucifix was hung above it. I passed beneath the archway, and stopped to look up at the depiction of Christ.

"Lord, why did your father give us free will?" A bite of bitterness was in my voice.

I heard a laugh behind me and turned to see the silhouette of a woman, in addition to the barrel of a shotgun pointed directly at me.

"I often wonder the same thing." She didn't lower the gun.

" Are you going to shoot me?"

" Well that depends."

"On what?"

"On whether you comply. Place any weapons you have on the floor."

"I have no weapons and I'm not a threat."

" No weapons? You approached in military jeep. You think I would trust you?"

"Why wouldn't you?"

"You're either a military operative or a civilian who stole a military vehicle. Either way, that rings alarm bells."

"I didn't steal a military jeep because I'm a threat. I was threatened."

Everything was silent for what felt like ages. She lowered the shotgun before walking over to the candle and matches that lay on the dining room table. She struck the match and lit the candle.

I remained still. I had no weapons and this

woman was armed.

She was in her mid 30's and had wavy ginger hair with fair features. She looked like a delicate creature, not the sort of person you'd expect to be pointing a shotgun at an intruder. I realized suddenly, I had no right to feel victimized. I was intruding and she had every right to display her aggression.

"I thought the house was empty. I've been trying to make my way to Texas, but ran into some trouble along the way at a military base. Things turned violent. I was scared. I met a soldier who gave me the keys to the jeep so I could escape unharmed." I don't know why I felt the need to explain myself, but she didn't stop me. "I've been driving without a sense of direction for a couple of hours. I needed a place to sleep, and this farm house was my spot of luck." I was crying again. "For God's sake." I sighed, wiping a tear from my eyes. "Please. Can I at least sleep in your barn for the night. I'll leave in the morning."

The nameless women walked over to me smiling "The more the merrier."

"You believe me?"

She nodded "The story's believable. You can spend the night here."

"My name's Maggie."

"Lily, " I answered.

25 Days After

Local Radio Broadcast

(A transcript taken from the emergency broadcast system)

This station has interrupted its regular broadcast programme at the request of the United States Federal Government. For the foreseeable future this station will remain on air to broadcast News

and official Information for areas assigned to them.

The following Message has been Received and Verified for your local area:

The authorities have received reports about bad weather in near by locations. They would like to warn local citizen that an electrical storm is expected to hit in the next couple of hours. This will cause serious destruction. Therefore citizens are advised to remain in their homes, until further notice.

This Please stay tuned for further announcements.

This Station has...

26 Days After

Mrs.Gallie and Dylan

I went into Mom's room to keep her company before going to bed. I had made a paper airplane, and decorated it with my pencils; creating the very first Gallie Airlines!

I came into the room and launched the plane into the air, it flew all the way to Mom's side.

She tried to prop herself up with her pillows, but seemed very tired so she stayed lying down. I sat next to the bed cross legged looking up to her so she could look down at me.

"Do you think Tamie will come by plane?" I asked.

"I don't think it would fit in the driveway", Mom responded.

I giggled at the joke and she sent a smile down to me. She reached to the plane and held it up to the ceiling so she could take a good look at it.

"It's very good, well done you. My little engineer", she smiled.

I looked up at my creation in her hand, she launched it across the room, I watched it glide and gradually and delicately land her dressing table.

"How far did it go?", she said exhaustively, with a brave smile.

"It went all the way to the dressing table" I declared, running to pick it up and to then rejoin my mother, plane in hand.

"How do you think Tamie's coming home?"

"By car maybe, or maybe shes found a coach of people?" she wondered.

I nodded, despite the unsure response, Tamie was definitely coming home.

She began to breath heavily, I reached for the inhaler under her bed but she managed to get her breath back.

"I hope that she'll be back soon, it would be nice to see her", she expressed, warmly with a slight quiver in her lip. I nodded, as I wanted to see Tamie too.

I looked back down at my plane. "I bet she is coming by plane, " I commented. "I think that she climbed a mountain to get above the ash cloud". Mother smiled and shut her eyes, but I knew she was still listening so I continued my story.

"On the mountain she found a plane, and right now she's flying over the ash cloud home", her smile began to fade away as she fell asleep. I picked myself up from the carpet and gave her a hug goodnight; before leaving her to my own bedroom.

"I love you mommy, " I whispered back to her before I left.

```
Tamie
```

The day would have been nice if the world hadn't ended. The sun shined through the ash more brightly than usual, allowing me to see the landscape a bit further ahead and in a bit more detail. The downside was the heat; it had to be over 100 degrees outside. The dry, suffocating air caused my body to ache, and the crowbar in my hand to leave scorching, red marks wherever it touched my skin. I needed gloves. I stopped for a moment, taking a sip of what little water I had remaining, when a set of headlights shined toward me through the dust. I quickly put away my water, and held my crowbar ready, as I continued to walk.

As the car and I grew close enough to be seen through the ash, the now visible heavy pickup came to a stop. Immediately, I thought of the young man with his throat blasted open in front of the shopping center. I didn't have the shotgun anymore, and my pistol wouldn't have been easy to get to this time. I didn't want any trouble, but if it came my way I needed something to protect myself with.

I walked forward, head down, hoping that when I passed the pickup the driver would just continue on their way. I leaned the crowbar against my shoulder, the metal stinging my bare skin.

The vehicle slowed as it came up beside me, and the window came down a crack. My body tensed, ready for a fight.

"You okay?" A man in his forties sitting behind in the driver seat asked.

I noted he was alone in the car, but I could see a baseball bat lying across the passenger seat. "I'm fabulous. I've always wanted to know what it's like the be dehydrated in the middle of one of the hottest areas in the country while humanity is on the brink of destruction. It's a very educational experience."

"Alright then. Sorry I asked." His soothing tone was a bit surprising, I hadn't expected kindness anymore.

He looked out his windshield, and then turned back to me and said, "Have you been into any shops recently, stranger?"

"Not recently, " I lied, not wanting to give away the fact that I had anything of value to steal. "The stores are mostly empty by now anyway."

"You must be hungry then, " he said to me. I didn't detect any threat in his words, and I slowly let myself relax a bit.

"You might as well come with me, " he suggested and gestured to the passenger seat where the baseball bat still lay, "C'mon, hop in."

A bit shocked, my body tensed again, "What? I'm not getting the car with some stranger old enough to be my dad."

"You misunderstand. I have a wife and children back home, and we have a basement full of food. You could use some food, right? And I'm sure you have plenty of skills that could help us around the house."

I thought for a moment. Looking into this man's eyes, I could see that he meant no harm. I could be wrong about him, but he was offering to feed me. I was sure I could defend myself against him if he did decide to try anything.

"Please, " he repeated, "My mother would be so disappointed in me if I left a young woman out on her own in a place like this."

He was persistent. He seemed good hearted, and as he said, I had experienced the wider world since the cloud had hit. I had better survival skills than an ex-white collar office worker who had holed up with his children.

I nodded my head just a bit, "Alright, I'll

come." I walked slowly to the other side of the car. He moved the bat as I opened the door and climbed in. The door made a heavy clunk as I slammed it shut beside me.

"I'm Rich, Rich Ward, " extending his hand toward me.

"Tamie, " I shook his hand.

* * *

We stepped through the front door, our presence announced by a jingling bell hanging just over the doorway, reminding me of the stores in old 50s movies. The foyer was open, and we were greeted by an ash covered rug atop slightly scuffed hardwood floors. Just before the staircase on my right was a tiled room with cupboards. On my left was a hallway with walls covered with various pictures in stylized frames.

From somewhere on the second floor I could hear notes singing off of an unseen violin. The sound made me smile. It was the first beautiful sound I'd heard since I left. My smile was interrupted by a tall, thin woman rushing into the foyer.

The woman had a fine bone structure with short, surprisingly well kept, blonde hair. She came with a smile that instantly faded when she saw me.

"I sent you out to get food, not something new to feed, " The woman glared at Mr. Ward and vaguely gestured at me.

"I found her walking alone on the side of the road. I couldn't just leave a young woman out there. It wouldn't have been right, " said Mr. Ward.

"Look at her, " the woman, I correctly assumed to be Mrs. Ward, growled. "Her hair's a mess, there's a crowbar in her hand, and I think that's blood on her clothes."

"For all you know that is her own blood, she could have been attacked."

"We don't know, she could have just-"

"Enough, " My tone was louder than I had meant for it to be. "I don't want to cause trouble. I just need somewhere safe and comfortable to rest. Fix my filthy hair, or cut it. I don't care. If you don't want me here at all, I'll just leave now. It's fine."

The couple stared at me briefly.

Mrs. Ward sighed. "Fine. But only a night or two."

I looked around cautiously again. I saw a small boy peeking around the top of the stairs. He had brown hair, but the same cheeky smile of small boy his age. Just like Dylan's. He spotted me looking at him and darted away, his cheeks turning red. The couple were still bickering quietly.

I nearly turned around and walked out, but the music stopped, and there was a clatter of feet came down the other set of stairs. There were two girls with the boy, one, the elder, was wheat blonde, and the other dark haired, but they had similar features. Mrs. Ward spotted me looking at them.

"Come down and meet our guest. She won't be staying with us long. Just like the other man, she will only be staying a little bit to get herself all fixed up." The children approached slowly and introduced themselves, the eldest, Millie, made a face at my appearance.

The other daughter Lola, seemed like she would rather have been doing something else, but the little boy, Chris, hugged me tightly.

"Get away Chris. She is all dirty. I don't want you getting ill. Go and wash your face and your hands now. With soap." The little boy looked shocked at the harshness of his mother's tone, but toddled off all the same.

"You'd better clean up too, I'll go and get you some clean clothes, they probably won't fit very well, but they'll be better than nothing." Her tone didn't really change when she spoke to me.

I thanked her politely. I could understand her fears, but one night wouldn't kill them or their children.

27 Days After

Dylan

    I stood in the middle of the road opposite the house, the sky was deep grey and I was being pounded by the heavy fall of the ash which gradually surrounded me, as if I were trapped in the eye of a tornado. Without my goggles it was hard to see through the ash, I attempted to cup my hand around my eyes, but the cloud was sting my eyes making me weep.

The estate was in ruins, the houses crumbling all around me. I turned to look at the house and watched the roof raise into the air, all of our stuff, all of our food and all my drawings were being sucked up by the ash cloud and tearing the house down so that nothing remained. Then I heard Mommy.

"Dylan", she called out. I looked up to the end of the road, it took me some time to adjust my eyes to the darkness but she stood as a shadow at the crossroads at the end of the street.

"Let's go find Mommy an inhaler, dear", and then she strode off down towards the shops, the way we always went to buy our weekly groceries. I ran after her following her shadow from street to street, but she was too fast for me to keep up. There were a number of moments where I had thought I'd lost her, but then she would call out to me,

"Dylan I'm over here", her voice was grainy

like the cassette tapes they play in school. Often I would find her at the end of the street from where I had just come from and I would have to go back. This was not our estate anymore, a mere labyrinth of the memories of my friends and neighbours.

I turned a sharp corner to find my mother standing there at the end of the street. In front of her was the corner of the world. She stood staring out into the ash cloud. Mom was not well and I had to get her to a safe place, but I still felt scared to call back out to her. She stood on the ledge, her toes hanging off the edge of the road and into the ash cloud.

I slowly paced forward, as I trying to scale the branch of a tree, or pick a flower on the edge of a cliff; and then I reached out and tugged upon the shadow cape of my mother's coat.

The cloak rotted away in my hand as I tugged, my mother turned around, screaming like a hound. I stood there frozen to the ash carpeted road.

Her face was rotting away like dried fruit, the skin peeling back, tight to the bone in stark contrast against her red, blood filled eyes.

Her neck flicked back as if she had been attacked by the ash cloud. She let out a heavy
groan as she vomited her terminal breath into the
storm. With her head still looking up into the
night sky, her eyes closed, she took a deep breath
and a stream of ash filled her lungs.

I cried out to her, and after a pause she turned
to face me; before jumping of the edge of the world
and into the ash.

I woke up with a scream, and holding Sebastian with a tight grip. Tears ran down my eyes
and I couldn't catch my breath. I looked for my
torch, which I eventually found next to my butter box boat' under some sugar paper. Turning
it on I pushed over the covers and ran straight to
Mommy's room to see that she was alright. Her
door was shut but so I used Sebastian to help me
open the brass handle.

I pushed open the door and ran to Mommy's
side.

She was leaning over the side of the bed for her

inhaler. I placed my torch down on her bedside table and went to pick up the inhaler for her. I thought that it was empty but I picked it up and join her in bed. I helped to prop a pillow up for her and then pulled one over for myself.

I pulled the sheets up over me and Sebastian and gave Mommy a hug, she was a bit cold, and she asked me to fetch her an extra blanket. I pulled myself and Sebastian from the covers, picked up my torch and went back to my room to find a blanket. I pulled an orange blanket from the drawer under my socks and pants and went to re-join Mom in her room.

I placed the blanket around her and she thanked me for it, and then asked if I was okay.

"No, " I whimpered pulling the sheets over me and Sebastian.

"I had a bad dream, " we hugged again and then she asked me to tell her what happened.

"The ash took you away from me." It took me a moment to find the confidence to her.

"Mommy's not going anywhere, she's here, with

you!"

Things will be okay, we had the bandana and scarf to keep the ash out; and the inhaler for emergencies. She held the inhaler in her hand. I smiled. The blue plastic of the inhaler was the most beautiful colour. I know, such a small refined thing, a life saviour. I wondered about getting one for my superhero's utility belt, but knew that Mom would make better use of it.

Tamie

The sound of Millie's violin could be heard above me mixing with the sounds of Mrs. Ward cleaning below. I walked slowly, looking around at the large, expensive house. I was surprised the place had been left untouched, because it wasn't very far off the main road. Although, I had noticed that the ash had cloaked it nearly completely, and the visibility out there was quite bad.

I went to Chris's room. His door was wide open. I looked in to see him sitting on a rug made to look like a two dimensional town. Various toys were strewn around the room.

His eyes meet mine and he asked, "Want to play?"

I smiled at him, and walked in saying, "Sure."

He points to the fire station on the map. "You sit there."

"Okay, " I noticed he was sitting on the police station.

He handed me a small plastic firetruck, and informed me, "That's you." Holding up a plastic police car that was missing a wheel he told me, "This is me."

I wheeled around the toy car where he told me to, making various sounds and voices as I did so.

The room was larger than a child his age would

need, and had many pieces of furniture that would have lasted him until he moved out on his own. The wallpaper was starting to peel through. It displayed a pattern of characters from the movie The Lion King. I couldn't help but think of Dylan.

I hadn't grown out of Disney movies before Dylan was born. I would sit up with him blaring whatever kids' movie I could get to play on the screen first, and hold him during the scary parts. He was too young to understand the stories, but he still enjoyed watching them with me. We watched The Lion King a lot. I nearly had the script memorized. He always wanted to watch the old Robin Hood as well. Between those two films, I had probably spent hundreds of hours sitting on the couch with my little brother.

"Tamie?" Chris tugged lightly on my hair, which brought me back. "You aren't listening, " He whined.

"I'm sorry. What were you asking, honey?"

"What makes your hair red like that?" He

fiddled with the tips of my hair.

I frown. "I was born with it. It's always been red."

"It's like a firetruck."

"Yes, it is."

"Or like Simba's."

"Yeah. Like Simba's."

I realize I shouldn't have been there. I shouldn't have been sitting in this house. I should be moving. I shouldn't have stopped moving. Dylan needed me. He needs me alive though.

I pick a place to put the fire truck on the map. "Want to race, Dyl... Chris, " I stutter.

"Yeah!" Chris rushes over to where I am, and we start to push the cars around making sounds. He didn't notice the couple tears run down my cheek.

Tamie

I sat at the table in the dining room, trying to imagine life before the disaster had never happened. For once, I wasn't imagining life with my family or with my friend, but memories of when I went with Dylan and Mom to Galveston two years earlier. I remembered walking onto that beach for the first time, curling my toes into the sand and feeling free. The memory was random. Still, it kept me going in those tough times.

Mrs. Ward was with me, but she said nothing. She was glancing at me occasionally, but wasn't communicating. I liked the quiet.

Millie dame into the kitchen, visibly unhappy, as usual. "I'm bored. There's nothing to do in this place."

"Darling, why don't you play some music? I thought you were very good when you played James something. Or was it Jack? No wait Johnny! That's it, Johnny Greenwood, " said Mrs. Ward.

"I'm bored of him now, " Millie replied

"What about Busch?"

"Nope."

"Goldstein?"

"No!"

"For goodness sake, girl. What do you want me to say?"

"I'm bored of playing music like that! I don't have the internet on the stupid computer and there are no more new tracks for me to learn anymore! I can't leave the house anyway, can I?" Millie was clearly frustrated.

"It's not my fault you can't leave here, " Mrs. Ward reminded her.

"Dad went out, and Tamie was outside for a long time before she got here!", Millie cried.

I started tapping my fingers against the table. I couldn't listen to this much longer. Their bickering was fraying my nerves.

Mrs. Ward fought back. "Well, that's wonderful, but that was earlier. Things have changed, Millie, and in these times you have keep a hold of what you have. You're still alive, and that's because we have kept you here."

Millie was clearly stressed by her mother's yelling, and Mrs. Ward was obviously in no mood for her unreasonable demands. Suddenly, I burst out, "Hey, enough! You're mother and daughter! I bet you a million other families wish they could still say that to each other. Just think of how lucky you are, both of you. I have a mother and little brother out there, and I can't say whether or not I'll be able to see them again."

"Don't interrupt us. You're a guest in this house, and you will behave like one, " Mrs. Ward said to me, and began to walk out of the room. She turned back for a moment and added, "I'm sorry about your family, " and then left.

Millie looked at me for a moment, then ducked her head and ran back upstairs. I let my mind return to pleasant memories, rather than those of fighting my father.

The Ward Family

Mrs. Ward switched off the bedroom light before getting into bed next to her husband, snuggling up to him in the dark.

"She can't stay here Rich, " she whispered in the darkness.

He rolled over to face her. "Where else can she stay?"

"I don't know, but we have children to look after. She is another mouth to feed and we don't know how long this is going to last. We have to look after us. Who knows what she is capable of? She is covered in blood; she might murder us in our sleep for all the food that you told her we have. And she has a crowbar. Who walks around with a crowbar?"

"If she stays she could help us out around the house. And if we feed her, she won't need to steal

our food. She can help us Liv. You're being unreasonable. Why would she kill us, there is more
food than she could take with her?"

"If she is downstairs then she has to come past
our room first to get to the other rooms, and there
is that floorboard that you made sure was creaky
so you knew when the children were going outside.
She'll have to go over that before she gets to the
children, so we can stop her, " Mrs. Ward insisted.

"We can't leave her to starve. When this all
blows over, then you'll see reason. If you left her
to starve you'd feel so guilty Liv, especially since
we are so lucky to have the resources and supplies
to help. It's the right thing to do. Chances are,
the blood is from protecting herself from someone
else. She seems like a nice girl. Liv, you're really
being ridiculous. She can probably help you round
the house, keep the children company, keep them
busy. You know how much Millie likes to play
with new people, and Chris seemed quite taken
by her."

"Chris is a 4 year old, he is quite taken by

anyone new." Mrs. Ward rolled over to face away from her husband. "I'm not happy about this Rich, but if you want her to stay and won't listen to me, then you had better keep a close eye on her."

"Darling, it will be fine." He snuggled up to her. "We can't leave her to starve."

28 Days After

Dylan

Mommy was still in bed, so I went to see if she wanted to make something to eat.

"Mommy, are we going to have breakfast?" She didn't move. She didn't answer.

The room was dark, and Mom must have slept in still thinking that it was bed time. I pulled open the curtains and let in the daylight. The ash was light, "like putting icing sugar over brownies", recalling to Mom of how we made brownies for the last bake sale at school. Smiling to Mummy I opened the window to get rid of the smell. The smell was odd I wondered if some food had fallen under the bed, she was always reminding me of what happens to food that was left out.

The ash was slowly coating the remains of Lily's grandma's house next door.

"Mom, when is Tamie coming back?", Mommy didn't reply.

"Do you want anything Mom?" With her eyes still tightly shut she told me that she was still tired and might eat later. Mommy said that I could have some of the dried food in her bag. So I carefully walked downstairs; and back into the kitchen, keeping quiet so not to disturb Mommy upstairs.

Micheal

Lily

I went outside the house to drink the coffee and watch the sunset. The small amount of sunlight was nice. I sat on the bench under the old oak tree. It wasn't far from the entrance of the house and faced Miller's flower garden.

"How strong the nature is, I am amazed to see how well it coped with the apocalypse". Some flowers still bloomed and are making the garden look beautiful and colorful. Between the wonderful flowers I found a delicate yellow lily, growing out of the dry, wilted earth. It happens to be my favorite flower. Mum, also used to love lillies, and that's why she named me Lily.

Every year, on my birthday she would put a yellow lily behind my right ear and Dad would blessed me and wished me all the best in the world. "I miss them so much!"

"I used to be so happy when I was around them."

I smelt the flower and touched its petals, picked it and put it behind my right ear. It brought a wide smile on my face and for a bit, I felt more hopeful about the days to come.

"I need to continue my journey, to Grandma's house." I said to myself, "There is still a long way to go and I need to get back on track."

Maggie comes outside and compliments the lily behind my ear and asks me if I know what a yellow lily signifies. "I don't know!" I answer, feeling embarrassed about my own ignorance.

It means "I'm walking on air"' It is like saying you are looking forward to being happy and having no worries'. "You will need to learn to let the other know your thoughts, Lily. It is the only way they can give you a hand. Everyone needs some help, from time to time" says Maggie, petting her on the shoulder...

The landing stairs of millers house were steep

and felt like a mountain to climb with this level of fatigue. The landing was extremely narrow for a farmers home, something I hadn't expected. I hadn't expected the house to be so clean, since personal appearances and cleanliness wasn't high on my list of priorities during the apocalypse. I guessed that being stranded in a house with nowhere to go was a good time to catch up housework.

The bedroom I slept in the previous night had a view of the front garden. There was old oak tree in front of the window and the light outside cast shadows of the branches into the bedroom. I found it strangely familiar. I was surprised that old oak was still standing.

The young boys came bouncing into the room. The older boy shouting "I'm gonna catch you" as he chased his younger brother. I smiled at them. I longed for the ignorance of childhood dreams and imagination.

Maggie smiled too and waved to the boys to stand next to her. They did and stood by their mother. The older brother resting a hand on the younger ones shoulder.

I waved "You two are very naughty young boys".

Seeing Michael who looked about eight made me think of Johnny. Dale took the boy and promised me he'd be safe. He didn't have to and it was a completely selfless act.

"Boys, it's time to do your homework." Maggie mothered them. I hadn't seen their father as far a I was concerned; it was just Maggie and her two boys. That must have been tough for Maggie to raise her children on her own.

Over the past two days, I helped Maggie dig up root vegetables and crops and helped to keep the house clean. She had explained to me that since the ash cloud any crops that grew above ground had died. So she could only grow root vegetables. They had no farm animals left since the pollution of the ash cloud had killed the cows and horses.

In the last days, we were living off vegetables which she cooked on a portable cooker the family used on camping trips prior to the apocalypse.

As Maggie prepared the best root vegetable

soup she could muster with the crop we had picked, I sat with Michael and Tom. They had so much energy. I had managed to sit them down nicely with a piece of paper and pen. We sat the dining room table drawing. Tom shot up stairs and came back down with a toy train.

"Can we draw this?" His eyes beaming with happiness.

"That used to be our Dads" Michael informed me.

"Used to?" and before Michael had a chance to reply Maggie reenter the room with the meal she had prepared.

Maggie explained that she did not fear the apocalypse because God will make sure her family will be safe. I understood from her confession that she was very religious and notice a large number of crucifixes around the house.

"Nobody eats until after grace" Maggie ordered.

She began:

For food in a world where many walk in hunger;

For faith in a world where many walk in fear;
For friends in a world where many walk alone;
We give you thanks, O Lord.'
We all finished with "Amen.".

Whilst in bed that evening the third line resonated in Lily's mind: For friends in a world where many walk alone.' Her family and friends had abandoned her either by their own choice or destiny.

She'd lost Dale and Johnny and but just as she thought she was alone and without hope she found the Millers.

There was not far too long until she fell into the most peaceful sleep thinking of the journey ahead of her.

Tamie

"Dinner's ready everybody, " Mrs. Ward called from the kitchen.

Slowly everybody assembled in the kitchen to see what she had been able to conjure up from the meager amount of cans that had been left in the cupboard.

"Millie, could you set the table for everybody, and Rich will you put Chris in his chair for me?" Glancing over to me, she said, "Tamie, please take a seat, it won't be too much longer."

I was starting to get a bit hungry myself. The meal Mrs. Ward had cooked up smelled pretty good. My stomach grumbled, and I hoped in the back of my mind that Mom and Dylan had enough food.

When the table was set, Mrs. Ward opened the oven door releasing a powerful smell of meat stew that made my stomach grumble loudly. Placing it triumphantly in the center of the table, she lifted the lid to show a thick gravy coating a few pieces of tinned corned beef and some little bits of canned vegetables. Next to it she placed a large bowl of instant mashed potatoes.

"I take it we've used the last of the potatoes from the garden then, " asked Mr. Ward.

"I'm afraid so. This was the best I could do this evening. Maybe you'll find some tinned ones next time you go out."

Mr. Ward noded.

"Well, who's hungry?" asked Mrs. Ward, retreating momentarily to the kitchen and retrieved a large serving spoon to scoop with. She was careful to make sure that her children got the best parts of the stew, giving the girls the majority of the meat and Chris an extra dollop of the mashed potatoes.

She then started to scoop some for herself and her husband making sure that they both received a bit of meat, and some vegetables, leaving primarily gravy in the bottom of the pan.

Mr. Ward looked over towards his wife, straight faced. He was fully aware that his wife didn't want me there, and her careful way of serving had not escaped his notice. To remedy the situation, when he received his plate from his wife he passed it straight to me. On receiving the plate of mashed potatoes and gravy that had been meant for me, Mr. Ward thanked his wife with a smile. With the last plate being served, all those around the table started to eat.

After pushing the meat around her plate for a while Lola started to complain,

"This meat tastes weird, Mom."

"Well, unfortunately that's all there is. It was this or tuna again, " responded Mrs. Ward in a tired voice.

"It's not so bad if if you mix it all together, Lola, " I offered. Mrs. Ward had clearly had enough, so I took it upon myself to encourage the girl to eat.

After a few mouthfuls, Lola decided that she had had enough and pushed her plate away from her. A couple of seconds later her father said, "Well if you're not going to eat it Lola, I'm certainly not going to see all that lovely meat go to waste. Slide your plate over this way will you?"

Mr. Ward quickly scraped the meat on to his plate and settled down to the rest of his meal.

Tamie

I was standing in a pitch black void. No sight, no smell, no feeling. White came, then grey. The ground beneath my feet returned, as I slowly raised my head. I was on the library steps, from here you could see the Student Union and the parking lot. No one was there. There was just grey ash and a desolate campus.

My heart pounded. The only sounds in this world came from within me.

I blinked. A slow deliberate gesture. When my eyes reopened the scene had changed. The ash descended upon me, forming into statues of Tamie and Dylan, Marcus, Annabelle, Maria, Dale, Johnny, Maggie and her boys. They stood at the bottom of the stairs static. No emotion. They were just sculptures. I took one step down towards them but as I did the ground around them shook. Another step taken. Dale's left arm fell to the ground and disintegrated into the haze. Being near anyone just hurt them, Tears threatened escape. I had to fight it. What would happen if I cried? A tear rolled down my cheek. As it fell from my chin, reality returned.

I woke with sudden panic. Smoke saturated the air. It felt like a hand was pressing down on my chest as the tendrils of smoke forced their way down my throat and into my lungs.

In the distance I heard a bang. Against the dizzying pain inflicted by the oxygen deprivation I stumbled towards the window. I opened it and saw a man and women stealing our provisions. The man was well built, he exposed a distinctive and ugly facial tatoo when he looked back, directly at me, and saluted.

I didn't have time to worry about these villains, I was no match for them. I let them take the food and water.

As my senses returned, with the cleaner air outside my window, I heard the weak cries of terrified children and Maggie's screams. I could see an orange glow beneath the door, the fire was spreading.

My fear took over. How could I save this family from a fire? I looked towards the window there was the tree directly outside. I knew that I could jump and make it out of the building. If I did so, I could leave unharmed. Fear took over completely. I threw myself at the tree, painfully landing in its branches. I climbed down. As my feet touched the floor I looked up to find the mother waving frantically, this returned my senses. That wasn't who I am.

Just below the windowsill of the dining room table stood a bench. A bench like the bench Tamie and I would sit on as we watched her younger brother Dylan when we took him to the park.

I ignored the pinch of emotion in my throat. I couldn't afford the distraction. Having ran to the door and entered the house, I found that the flames had engulfed it almost entirely. I took a step back, the heat bring tears to my eyes. A photo of the family lay on the floor across the room. I tried to retrieve it, but by the time I picked it up Michael and Tom's faces had been removed by the flames. Only the mother remained.

Throwing away the remains of the picture, I ran towards the door. The flames were closing in, cutting off my only exit. I had no choice. I rushed through the flames. My sleeve catching on fire when I did so. I fell to the floor rolling over in attempt to put it out, I barely succeeded. My arm was seriously burned, but I had to ignore the pain. I hurried over to the kitchen table, where I had left the key to the Jeep. If I parked it beneath the mother's window she could jump onto the roof.

I ran as quickly as possible out of the fire and to the barn. Luckily it wasn't too far away. I opened the door and stuffed the keys in the ignition. I felt the rumbling of the engine roaring to life. It was in tune with my motivation. The pain in my arm was the last thing on my mind as I drove, Maggie was still in there.

I exited the Jeep and looked up at her. "Jump onto the roof of the jeep!"

She hesitated, but jumped, cringed as she landed.

I gave her my hand and helped off the roof of the car.

"My children!" she gasped, " My Chil...My..." She struggled to battle the choke hold her emotion had over her throat.

They were still in house.

"Attic" I heard her weak trembling voice. Since the ash cloud the mother thought it would have been safer for the boys to stay in the attic where the air was clearer.

Maggie's expression changed, it turned hard instead of panicked. She ran towards the door.

I knew she'd die if she attempted to save her children, I didn't have time to think.

Maggie may have wanted to die in that fire

with her children but I didn't allow her to. I tackled her to the ground and held her. She fought, and was strong. I had to be stronger. She struggled, screamed, and cried. We heard Tom and Michael screaming in agony as the flames devoured them.

When their tortured cries ceased. Maggie stopped struggling, before letting out an anguished cry, like the howl of an injured animal. It echoed in the darkness of the farm and will forever echo in my mind.

Maggie began to shake. Her body threatening to fall apart. I had to hold the pieces together. She must have resented me at that moment, but she didn't turn on me. I sat holding her as we both stared at the burning remains of her life.

"I want to bury them"

"Maggie, they were in the attic. We wouldn't be able to find their remains amongst the rubble." I heard my voice and was disgusted by its cold nature. That wasn't a time for logic. I knelt to face her. "Besides. I don't feel that seeing their remains will help you."

I could hear the hunger of the flames, the crackling. I stared into her eyes, red with tears, I could see a reflection of the flames dancing over the house. Silence continued as we watched the house fall apart. Leaving only the wooden beams of the structure and brick of the foundation.

Maggie approached the house, walking through what remained of the doorway. I followed and stood next to her. Tears flowed as we both cried. We wouldn't find the boys. Maggie clambered over rubble searching for something. Something to hold onto. I remained static unsure what to do. Maggie returned to me holding a toy train.

Tom had wanted draw the train.

31 Days After

Dylan

I looked through Mom's rucksack for some food for me and Mom, I found a large bag and pulled out two tins of plums, Mom told me to save the peaches for the weekend. I grabbed some spoons and ran back upstairs to share with her. The room was a little stale, but I assumed it just to be the weather outside.

"Hi Mom, I brought up the plums you asked for", I sat next to her in bed and opened the tin and began to eat them, they were sweet and made a nice change to the bags of cashew nuts we had been eating for the last few days.

Having drunk the syrup from the can I looked out of the window, much of the window was covered with ash and we were unable to see outside, but the corners of the window were bear letting us look out into the grey sky.

I place the tin can on top of a book on Mom's bed table and then walked to the window. I wanted to open it, and feel the breeze on my skin, but Mom told me not to, so I closed the curtains.

Suddenly the room became very dark, "I'll just go fetch my flashlight", I declared leaving her room.

I found my flashlight next to Sebastian, "Howdy Sebastian", I greeted him and then went back to rejoin Mommy.

I turned on the torch entering her room and

placed it on the end of the bed, but the room was still dark. I tried placing it next on her washbasket and again on her bedside table but we were not satisfied with the lighting.

Mommy suggested that I placed it on the dressing table, firstly this didn't change anything but as I stood the torch I found that the light reflected off from the mirror lighting up the room.

"Look at that Mommy", I exclaimed in astonishment. She told me that I had done a good job, and so rejoined her in bed.

I opened a second tin of the plums, Mom said that she was very exhausted and so asked me to feed her, just as she used to feed me. "OK", I replied with a smile, "I'll look after you". I picked up a segment of plumb onto the spoon and brought it to her mouth.

The plumb fell of the spoon leaving reddish juice stains on her and her pyjamas.

She told me that she wasn't hungry and said that I could have the plums, I picked up the segment she dropped and put it in my mouth.

"Are you sure?" I asked hesitating over the tin of plums; but she told me that she insisted so I sat with her until bedtime eating the plums and talking about when we would next go out.

32 Days After

Tamie

Mrs. Ward passed me by. I was sitting and playing with Lola and Chris as she dusted, in some game we made up. She smiled briefly, maybe I was starting to grow on her. Maybe even she thought that I would be a good influence on the children, never even swearing in front of them.

She dusted one room at a time, ignoring that everything would be just as bad again the next day, or next hour.

I heard her sigh at my room, she probably didn't like the mess of my clothes and a few other belongings. "Nobody's perfect I guess.", I heard her mumble to herself as she started to organize the room.

"It must just be a toy. A fake. A bluff." When I heard her say that, I felt my heart sink.

I heard a loud bang, then she cried, "It's real!!!"

"Tamie! Tamie! I need you here, now!".

I stood slowly hearing Mrs. Ward call me. "I'll be right back. Your Mommy needs me." I smiled at the children.

I walked up to find Mrs. Ward holding my gun and its magazine. "What is this?"

"A gun. I needed it to defend myself."

"You didn't tell us."

"It didn't cross my mind."

"Don't make excuses!"

"What's going on?" I turned around to see

Millie eyeing the gun.

"Go watch your brother and sister." I squeaked.

When Millie was gone, Mrs. Ward growled. "That wasn't your place."

"Reflex."

"We will discuss this when Rich gets home." She tried to leave the room with my gun.

I grabbed my crowbar and stopped her. "Gun stays. Or else."

Mrs. Ward turned pale, but obeyed before storming off.

*　　　*　　　*

Mr. Ward stepped in quick with a smile that instantly faded when he saw Mrs. Ward and I.

"What's going on?"

"The office. Now." Mrs. Ward stomped into the nearby room.

Mr. Ward and I locked eyes briefly, but said nothing.

When the door was closed, Mrs. Ward started to yell. "Did you know she had a gun?"

"Gun?" Mr. Ward looked at me quickly.

"Yes the gun she snuck into our home. The gun she probably planned to kill us with."

"I was never going to hurt your family." I growled. "I'm not a monster!"

"Could have fooled me with that crowbar of yours." Mrs. Ward scoffed.

"Can someone explain to me what happened?"

"She not only hid the gun, but threatened me with her crowbar."

I made a fake laugh. "Feels like a fucking soap. I warned you not to take it, I will need it out there."

"You did know, didn't you Rich?"

"Liv, I didn't know."

"None of you knew. I kept it a secret since I didn't know if I could trust you. Then I never told you for this exact reason."

"Where did you get a gun?" Mr. Ward looked at me.

Mrs. Ward scoffed. "Probably was in some gang and already had it when everything started."

"Liv."

"I was in University, I wasn't lying about that. I got the gun from a dead police officer when all this started. I took his car too."

"That's a reasonable explanation. We might have done the same thing." Mr. Ward smiled weakly at me. "You should have told us about the gun though. That's not something you should have hid."

"She has to leave." Mrs. Ward's voice went quiet. "Gather your things and leave. Right now! Take your evil little gun with you!"

We all stood quietly, so quiet I could hear my own heart pumping my blood.

Mr. Ward stared at the floor, frowning. Mrs.

Ward glared at me, barely blinking. I fingered the edge of a corner table that used to hold a potted plant.

"I'll go. I've stayed put too long anyway. I need to get to Dylan." I walked toward the door. "I'll get my things."

Mr. Ward stopped me. "Tamie. Leave in the morning. It's getting late. Rest here tonight and leave tomorrow."

"No." Mrs. Ward rushed over. "Now. She leaves now."

"Liv, putting her out at dark and expecting her to get a good distance away is unreasonable. She's still just a girl."

Mrs. Ward sighed. "Fine. The moment it is light out, she's out. No more discussion."

"Alright." Mr. Ward smiled. "I get you a few bottles of water and some food."

"No." Mrs. Ward's voice went shrill. "She betrayed us. I'm not giving her anything else."

"But Liv."

"No."

I sighed. "Enough. No food and water, means no food and water. You won't be able to convince her otherwise. I'm not family. She doesn't care if I live or die."

Before the two can say anything else I was on the stairs. The children watched me on the second floor, I knew they'd heard.

I needed food and water though. All I had of my own supplies left was cheap pasta. I had to steal some supplies that night when I left.

33 Days After

Local Radio Broadcast

This Station has interrupted its regular broadcasting programme at the request of the United States Government. For the foreseeable future, this station will remain on air to broadcast news and official information for areas assigned to them.

The Following message has been received and

verified for your local area:

The local authorities would like to make local citizens aware that electrical storms overnight have lead to severe fires in the local area. The local authorities would like to strongly recommend that local citizens remain in their homes as the aforementioned fires have added to the already high pollution levels outside.

This Concludes Please stay tuned for further announcements.

This Station ...

difficult for individuals to move.

34 Days After

Dylan

I went into Mom's room, it was cold, the weather had changed from this morning. I noticed that I had left the window open so I quickly went to close it and apologized to Mom for forgetting to shut it. She was slumped over, she said she wasn't feeling very well.

"I'll help you backup", Mommy was stiff, "I'm sorry I forgot to close the window", she assured me it was okay as I hugged her, she was very cold so I pulled a blanket up around her.

"Mom, I think we're going to have to go shopping again soon", I noted without reply.

"We've only got a few things left, your bags getting empty".

But Mommy wasn't well, and said that we should leave it for a later time.

"Shall I make you some apple and parsnip soup? That's the one Tamie always makes me when I'm not well?" Mom reminded me that we didn't have any in, but thanked me for offering.

I went and sat next to Mommy in bed, to help her try to feel better, "I made you this", I declared revealing an orange card I had made for her. On the top I had written Get Well Soon Mommy', and underneath I had drawn the two of us fighting of the ash, and inside a picture of us both eating peaches.

I placed the card on her bedside table and

reflected upon Tamie. "I remember when I had the chicken pox", I looked up at Mommy resting, "I remember Tamie made me soup every day, or most days, I can't remember. My favourite day was apple and parsnip".

I looked back at the card I had made Mommy and wondered when we would next brave the clouds.

"Do you think Tamie will make me apple and parsnip soup when she comes home?", I asked looking back up at Mommy; but she had fallen asleep. So I got out from the bed closed the curtains and left the room to see Sebastian.

Lily

Nearly a week had passed since the fire and

I'd learned a lot about Maggie. She had inherited the farm from her father. As a child, her father taught her how to fix their tractors; she loved anything that ran with a metallic heart. The idea of building up machines intrigued her as a child. Her dream was to leave the farm behind and study at University. Yet, she felt she needed to keep the family farm running in memory of her father.

Part way down the road the military jeep ran out of gas and we continued our trek on foot. It seemed most logical to follow the free pass and try to escape by continuing her journey away from the darkest cloud of ash.

I had started to feel sick, and the unbearable heat made the situation worse. Found my arm either ached, or stung unbearably. My skin had started to turn strange colours. It wasn't long until the infection became extremely painful.

The haze today wasn't too difficult to see through which meant we could see a stranded individual looking into the engine of his car. I was half tempted to walk past the car and the male but

Maggie noticed his distress. She started walking to the man.

"Sir, are you alright ?" she asked.

"Do I look alright?" he replied. "I'm sorry. That was rude of me" He then apologised. He was a dusky skinned man, in his late 20's and had a gorgeous smile. He was tired which was obvious from the bags beneath his eyes. When he smiled faint wrinkles appeared next his eyes.

He left the car and introduced himself to us.

"My name is Tim" he extended an arm out to Maggie

"Maggie" she replied and they shook hands. Tim turned to me.

"Lily" I announced. He offered his hand and as I went to shake his hand I winced at the pain.

" That's a nasty burn you have there."

I nodded.

"May have a look?"

"Do you know what you're looking for?" I asked.

"I'm a pharmacist and I've took professional

classes in first aid" He smiled back.

I had a feeling this must have been a habit he picked up from his profession. Who in their right minds would be smiling in these times. Regardless he calmed my nerves. "okay".

" I noticed you have car trouble " Maggie interjected. "whilst you're looking at her burn would you like me to check the engine?"

He looked surprised. Either at the offer or the fact that Maggie knew about cars.

"Well?" She asked again.

"Yes, that would be great but I have no idea how to fix it"

Tim explained, "The engine is overheating and keeps on stopping in order for it to cool down."

In the distance I heard Maggie singing to herself as she inspected the vehicle. I noted that she had a lovely voice. The song wasn't familiar but I'd be sure to ask her what song it was in the future.

"I'll be back in one second" Tim quickly stated and strode back to the car.

I stood there listening to Maggie's singing. Maybe the song was a lullaby she just to sing to her boys.

Tim returned with a number of medical supplies.

"May I ?" requested Tim.

I nodded and lifted my arm towards him.

He soaked cotton balls with the rubbing alcohol and began to clean my wound. I closed my eyes and breathed deeply against the pain.

"There, I think I've sterilised the wound as best as I can" he continued "To be sure that there is no chance of infection use this antibiotic cream."

I took the tube and looked at the label, it read "Sulfamylon". " Where do medical scientists get these names?" He laughed but didn't give an answer.

Maggie tells us that the car is ready to go now however, she needed to use the remaining water we had in order to fill in the coolant reservoir tank. The car should work properly for a while however, it may happen for the engine to overheat again in a couple of hours.

Tim looks panicked hearing Maggie's diagnosis because he will not be able to fix the car if he will broke again. I notice it and offer for both to accompany him. He accepts and thanks us for the help provided.

So, we start the journey again and continue to drive along the freeway.

* * *

I am staying in the right front seat of the car and Tim is driving. We have all the car windows open and AC on full speed to help air the engine and make sure it won't overheat too soon.

I noted that Tim kept

"So, what's your story, Lily? Who are you? And where are you going now?" asks Tim clumsy.

"I do not know who I am anymore nor where I want to go." I replied with an upset voice.

"Ok, then what are you running from?" asked Tim curiously.

"What do you mean?" "What makes you think I am running from something?" and I frowned at him.

"I am just trying to start a conversation, Lily", Tim smiles.

I looked at him for a couple of seconds and smiled back. I thought to myself that this was neither the time and place to have a crush on guy. For a moment, it seemed that Tim managed to save me from my depressing thoughts.

"So, what are you running from, then?" I made some courage and asked him.

"Let's say I just want to stay alive.I am not ready to die just yet. I still have lots of things to do and experiences to try out, people to love and last but not least, learn more about myself."

Impressive. Good answer.' I responded I see...'

I am returning home. Actually, to my Grand-mother's house and also want to check on my friend and her family, too. I just hope they are all alright, I can't lose them. They are the only family I have.", I confessed.

"I hope they're alright." Tim tried to encour-age me. At that moment, Tim received a call from a colleague giving information about the location of a safe military base where people went to until the dust grey clouds disappear.

We were reaching a crossroad where we need to follow different paths for the rest of their journey. I was still eager to go home and try to find out if the people I love are safe, the only people that I can call family'.

"Are you sure you do not want to come with us? You might have a dangerous journey ahead of you." Tim was trying to convince me to stay with them.

"Lily, I'm sorry but I can't go with you. I'm gonna go with Tim to the military base." Maggie tells me, "I think it will be safer there for now. Come with us, please it's safe and there's food, water and shelter."

"Are you sure, Lily?" Tim asks her again.

"No. I have to go back there, my grandmother, my friend" I shook my head and headed out.

"How in the name of God, are you going to survive in this?" Tim ran to me and caught my hand.

"Look! I'll manage, and if no at least I tried." I protested. "My grandmother needs me there."

"That's stupid and suicidal. What if they haven't made it? What are you going to do then?" he grabs my arm, he looks at me then sighs, "Look, at least take something for the road."

He handed me a small bag and shook my hand,

"Well hopefully we'll meet again."

The two of them drove off, looking down at the small bag I opened to find food, water and medicine, but also Tim's business card it read:

It is not our circumstances that define us, it is our response to circumstances.

I smiled and took it as a sign from fate, and I walked through the ash, to get home.

35 Days After

Local Radio Broadcast

This Station has interrupted its regular broadcast programme at the request of the United States Government. For the foreseeable future this station will remain on air to broadcast news and official information for areas assigned to them.

The following message has been received and

and verified for your local Area:

The authorities would like to remind all citizens to remain inside their homes. The authorities would also like to remind the citizens that if they cannot avoid leaving their homes that they should take extra precautions to protect themselves against the abrasive nature of the wind. Such as face masks and protective eyewear.

This concludes our broadcast. Please stay tuned for further announcements.

This stat...

36 Days After

Dylan

I walked into the room with two cans of peaches and two spoons for me and Mom. The smell in the room was getting worse, I wondered if it might be the bed sheets. Mom had told me that you should always try and change them at least twice a week. But my sheets hadn't been changed and hadn't gotten that bad.

I went up to her with the cans, I tried to place a tin into her hand but her fingers we're stiff, her skin was yellowing with a greenish tinge. "Mommy?" I held her cold hand hopefully, and dropped the can of peaches.

I looked upon her with sober eyes and saw her blistered dry skin. Her face was coated in frothing blood, that had run down her nose and into her dry breathless mouth.

I did not realise how long my mother had been like this; it must have happened around a week ago upon reflection, but at the time it was as if she had only just died.

I sat with her for a few hours, tears seemed to fall down my cheeks throughout the entire time that I was sitting next to her. I picked up one of the tins of peaches but couldn't eat them. I slept with Mommy for the last time that night.

Tamie

I carefully folded my spare cloths, making sure they took up as little space in the bag as possible. "I need" I whisper, "food and water." I go to put the pistol in my bag but stop. I put the pistol in the waist line at the back of my jeans instead. "Of course food and water. More specific. More water than food. Canned fruit, it has less salt. Will still need some beans or spam. I can't survive well on just canned fruit." I put the crowbar in the bag, and the knife in an easily accessible pocket. "Don't make me use this stuff. I should try to get some canned veggies. Corn or peas or something."

I carried my bag out, I thought it would be quicker to fill it if I didn't have to take it off my back. I move carefully past Millie and Lola's rooms. A floorboard creaks slightly, but the house falls back into silence afterward. The first set of stairs I get by without much sound. After the carpeted stair, the hardwood under my shoes seems to shake the house as I walk. I come to the highest risk rooms, Chris' and Mr. and Mrs. Ward's. Chris might be awake, or sleep more lightly. He also wouldn't be quiet if he finds me. Mrs. Ward might be listening, and might try to kill me if she finds me. I make it too the next set of stairs safely, without hearing anything from either room. The ground floor is easy, and I'm in the basement without a worry.

The first thing I spot is a pack of matches. It hadn't occurred to me to have something to start a fire. Without a thought I slip two packets into my pocket.

I go for the water next. Right as I take a bottle off the shelf I hear Millie's voice. "Tamie?"

I spin around, the teenage girl is standing on the stairs. "What are you doing down here?"

"I was thirsty, was just going to have a tiny bit of water. Didn't think your parents would mind."

"Why do you have your bag then?"

"Umm, I decided to put my last box of pasta down here. So everything would be together."

"You don't need an entire bag for that."

"Your right. I don't. Didn't even occur to me, probably just tired."

"You're stealing from us."

"Yes."

"Why?"

"I have to. You heard my argument with your mom. I need to go and-"

"Mom was right. You're just a dirty, evil, liar!"

"Millie, I'll die if I don't have any food or water out there. I need it to survive."

"Then go to the store or a soup kitchen, dad said the army would be trying to help too. Or just stay here."

"It's not that simple Millie. The blood on my top, that happened when everything started. A man attack me, tried to take all of my supplies. Things are even worse now."

"Aren't you doing the same thing?"

"No. I just wanted enough to get me by for a few days."

"Then you know there is somewhere you can survive."

"You don't get it. Damnit. You're oblivious to everything happening out there. Oblivious to the real world. Your mom is just an idiot spreading her stupidity to her fucking kids." I rushed up the stairs, pushing Millie aside.

"Where are you going?"

"I might as well be well rested for when I die of thirst."

As I walked from the doorway, I can hear Millie crying in the basement. I pause, but then keep going. I wasn't willing to apologize for telling her the truth.

Tamie

I sat in my room fiddling with whatever I could, I really must have upset Millie. I was, fiddling a box of matches, sliding it open and closed. "I need to go".

I walked down the stairs quietly to the basement to get some things, but this time I found a batch of floorboards that creaked loudly. I continued walking for a few more steps and stopped. "What has she done now?", I heard. Millie must have mentioned the earlier incident to her parents. It was time to leave.

Plunged into a state of panic, instead of going to the basement, I went back to my allocated room. "What should I do, distract them? sistract them."

I took a match, and set the curtains on fire. Just a curtain. The first match snapped. The second lit as I hoped. And to accelerate the fire? There was a can of deodorant, on the shelf next to me. I grabbed it and immediately began to spray the curtain. I smelt like fake strawberries. The fire erupted up to the ceiling. I jumped back in fright. It was the first time I had a been so close to flames of this magnitude.

Without thought or a word I ran out of the room and down the stairs to the ground floor of the house. Then I heard the parents' shocked reaction and hustling, because now they had noticed what I had done. My heart was pounding so heavily that I could feel each beat inside my ribcage.

"Kids, get out of the house!" "There is a fire!"

There was now probably just a minute or two before the building became impossible to stay in, now I needed to collect as many supplies as I could. There were still dozens of cans and boxes of groceries around the basement. I ran in and from a chest-level high shelf, scooped several items with my hands in an attempt to get them into my bag. Many fell in but others landed on the dark, dusty floor with a bang.

"I'm in luck", I cried breathlessly. There was a rucksack within reach and I simply dropped another batch of food and also water. Once again, some containers fell harmlessly into the sack, other slipped out of reach, now on the floor.

Sweating in deep fear for the house collapsing on top of me, I realized I was still grabbing the matchbox in my greasy hand, and I dropped that too.

Thankfully I had found some water bottles, those eventually would be very useful. They went in as well.

I roughly knew where the exit door was. As I found it, I could hear screaming from Chris and Lola. My room must have been fully aflame at this point. I froze and then the stairs collapsed and I heard more screams. There was no hope of a straightforward exit for them now.

My first instinct was to run along the side of the house. I saw what I identified as the road and kept running. And running. And running. And running.

By the time I stopped to catch my breath and turn around, the fire was just a dim glow on the horizon, as the haze had blocked a clear sight of the house. Although I couldn't see them anymore, I could still hear them.

"Help."

One of the children was screaming like a frightened animal. The sound of it drilled through my head into the deepest part of my mind.

"Please, somebody help."

One of them shouted into the darkness. Who were they screaming for? I was the only one there, and I wasn't going back.

One by one their voices slowly died out. There were no more shouts for help. Then there were no more shouts at all until the only voice left was the monstrous screaming of one of the children, and after a moment that too faded.

I could see and hear the flames licking up and over the walls, which strained and creaked. It seemed as though other parts of the house were collapsing, the chimney, the roof. They were dead. The Ward family had been killed, it was certain. The best they could hope for was that someone jumped from a window and escaped, at least one of the children, hopefully. But whether it were Chris, Lola, or Millie, they would be stranded and orphaned.

All I could think of doing was running as fast as possible from the crime scene again, not that anyone would care about it. My heart was full of grief and guilt, my head overflowing with terror. I sobbed wordlessly, absolutely shattered and scared stiff. Within that sensible estate, I had insulted the family living there, stolen from them and murdered them all through sheer selfishness and arrogance.

"My god, what have I done?".

I whimpered as all of my emotions faded into the ashes.

37 Days After

Tamie

My eyes were closed, but the heat had woken me up. My body was sticky with sweat, and the air moved with difficulty through my dry throat. The hard ground beneath me was unfamiliar, it felt as though I hadn't slept on hard ground in ages. My eyes opened slowly and I shoved my blanket, drenched with sweat, off of me. I grabbed my freshly procured backpack and checked its contents: four bottles of water, a couple cans of food including a can of peaches I could save for Dylan. I swallowed down a bottle of water before checking my tattered old bag, containing a few more bottles of water and various boxes of food grabbed in haste.

I shook the empty bottle of water over my mouth, causing a few drops to land on my still dry tongue.

"I should have grabbed more water, " I sighed, but quickly realized that there was no around to hear me, that's when it hit me.

Without warning, their voices tore through my mind. I remembered every scream and every cry for help. I had killed them. I had set fire to the Ward's house, and I had killed them. My thoughts raced, and I couldn't get the image of the fire glowing through the darkness and ashes out of my mind. Why had I done this? What possibly could have warranted such violence?

I pulled the pistol out and looked at it with disgust. That is why I had done it. I could have just told them. There was no need to keep secrets. They would have helped me and given me whatever I needed, but I had decided that this was more important. How stupid of me!

I can't change the past. I did what I had to do. It was me or them. If it was me, it might also have been Dylan. I was left without a choice. If only Millie hadn't found me in the basement, but she did.

39 Days After

Lily

My head began to spin, I couldn't when I last had a drink of water. The thought of water brought my own memories of water mirages on the road in hot summers past. Then my mind drifts to back when Mrs. Gallie was driving us to an amusement park. On the road, Dylan was fascinated by the mirages of water on the pavement. He begged their mom to pull over so he could see the water. The road wasn't busy so she obliged. Tamie and I took him out to see the fake water. He was mystified and the rest of the ride was spent trying to explain the illusion to the toddler.

With anyone else, Tamie would have lost her patients in explaining something like that, but she never lost her temper or got mad with Dylan. Only frustrated when he scared her.

Even when we were kids and I was visiting grandma, she was hard to play with. She was quite, short tempered, and moody. When I found out about her dad I understood. She was always smart though, and how she acted with Dylan, I knew she was a wonderful person. I knew she would still be alive if I've made it this far.

She showed me her true colours after my parents died. I was crying on the stairs, everything seemed hopeless. She came in, I had forgotten to close the door, and sat down next to me.

"They'll want you to live your life. Eventually

you will. Things will get better."

"How could you know?"

"I can't. I'm just guessing." She hugged me
then. "You can talk to me anytime. II might not
be much help, but I'll try. Besides it will make
you feel better."

After this I became part of their family. I spent
most my time at Tamie's, helping with Dylan or
watching movies, and sometimes even just talking.
Though it was mostly just me just talking while
Tamie listened. Mrs. Gallie became my second
mother when she was around, Tamie became my
sister, Dylan my little brother.

Before that, we first became real friends when
I found out our high school was starting a fencing
club. I was excited, always want to do the sport,
she had a slight interest and way the only friend
that was willing to go with me. Tamie wasn't very
enthusiastic about it, but we got paired together.
I didn't put my helmet on quiet right and she was
a bit clumsy with her foil.

Tamie hit me in the neck by accident, making a

cut. It wasn't bad, but it bled a lot. When Tamie saw what she had done, she started to panic. She became very distressed, and began to cry, she kept apologizing but was scared to get close to me. She never went back, but I joined the team.

I brought my hand to the faint scar, and the dryness of my throat reminding me of the lack of water.

Ahead of me I see a figure in the ash, some sort of mound, but the area should be flat. As I drew closer, I saw that it was a scrap heap. Some mopeds were strewn at the base of it. I decided to check them, and managed to get one of them running with a little rewiring. I had no water, but at least I didn't have to walk for awhile.

Tamie

My flashlight illuminated the dust in front of me as I staggered forward.

If they had kicked me out without any food or water, I'd be dead. Not directly, but they'd have killed me. Probably wouldn't even have given a shit. Wouldn't have even thought about the fact they would be killing Dylan too. They forced me. I wasn't trying to kill them, it just happened. Even if I had saved the kids, Millie might have come after me, the other two would die without parents. I couldn't take care of all of them and keep moving like this. In one place maybe, but I couldn't just forget Dylan.

I stopped in my tracks at the sound of growling. Nothing moved, but the growling happened again. Followed by a bark, like a puppy's. I take a few steps forward, slowly with my crowbar ready. A female coyote lays in my path, with four puppies huddled around her in the cold night air.

The mother raised her head slightly and growld, her body twitched upward but immediately slacked back down. I noticed her muzzle has fresh blood on her teeth, and a bit of dried blood was in the sand.

"You're lungs are failing. You've been completely poisoned."

The coyote tried to bark, but it came off as more of a wheeze.

"You just keep trying. You know damn well you can't protect them, you can't even protect yourself, but keep trying anyway. Probably haven't been able to for awhile, and you just lucked out so far. Just like Mrs. Ward. She was just like you. Letting her instinct overcome her better judgment. You're puppies are going to die, and you know it."

The coyote finally stopped moving, just lying with her eyes on me while her breaths came slowly. I come close, the puppies eying me expectantly. The mother's eye burns with the desire to kill me, protect her puppies.

I put the coyote out of her misery, and looked to her puppies. "You're mother might be inedible for all I know. You're going to die, but probably aren't toxic yet. I'll make it quick."

I made sure they each died in one strike.

With the remaining matches I started a fire, and after using my knife to clean them, as best as I could, I impaled them on some branches.

I roasted the meat over the fire. It ended up charred, and tasted like crap, but filled me up.

As I lay down to sleep, my thoughts found themselves on the Ward children. Mainly Chris' smiling little face. "I couldn't have done anything. His mother's stupidity doomed him." With my stomach full I drifted off to sleep with ease. I didn't have a single dream that night, normally I dreamt of Dylan and the old world, but not that night.

42 Days After

Dylan

I found myself lost in ash covered dreams. The nightmare is inescapable. The ash haunts the day and the night. I was lost in amongst the ash clouds. They were more violent than I had ever dreamt them before. I raised my hand up into the ash and it disappeared in the the darkness. I was standing in the middle of the road of my street recognising the texture of the road underfoot. I was scared, and the ash burnt my skin as it hit me. I attempted to cover my face by lifting my coat over my head, but much of the ash burnt through.

Around me I could hear cries and shouts of my friends and family; of Mommy and Tamie, of my school friends and teachers, of my neighbours, and my enemies.

"Come on Dylan, time to line up, " called Mrs. Dean.

"Dylan look at this. I found a frog!" called Thomas.

"That's a beautiful drawing, Dylan, " called Mommy.

"Time for a bath Dylan, " called Tamie.

"How's it going boy?" laughed Dad.

I walked through the ash cloud trying to locate Mom's voice when I found the door to the house.

The door opened as I walked up to it. I hesitated but the whistles of the ash storm behind me encouraged me to walk in.

I stood in the entrance and heard a banging from the living room. I ran into the room and found the corpses of my school friends, Thomas and Matthew, attacking the other Tamie. Tom and Mat were biting into Tamie's flesh, ripping out chunks of her body and eating them. Her screams were full of dread, but she was not the real Tamie.

"You're not my Tamie!" I yelled and slammed the door falling back into the entrance hall way..

A bang came from the dining room, I knew I had to investigate. It was the purpose of the dream.

The banging grew faster and louder as I walked up to the dining room door, as I opened it a man stood behind the dinner table. It was some sort of man, only surrounded by ash and the little light that was in the room appeared to be absorbed by the mystery figure. Slowly the figure raised a hand and walked through the table towards me.

I immediately ran from the room and back out

of the house into the ash clouds of the street. I
turned around to see the figure running behind
me, his hand outstretched and attempting to catch
me. Suddenly my face behind me I bannged into
the front door of the house, I had run directly from
it and found myself back at the house. I pushed
open the door and slammed it straight behind me.

I paused to catch my breath, but I soon heard
a banging from upstairs. I immediately knew that
it was coming from Mom's room. I ran up the
stairs to her room, tears running down my face I
could feel the tears burning my skin. I shut the
door behind me and stopped.

The room was humid and smelt of rot but her
body was gone. A banging noise came from somewhere in the room but I struggled to locate it. I
searched through her cupboard and under the bed
but both were devoid of anything. I looked around
the room, behind her curtains, in the drawers of
the bedside table, and then I saw Mommy.

I looked up at the mirror of her dressing table
and noticed that I did not have a reflection, but

Mom did and was clearly lying in bed.

I walked up to the mirror, to get a better view of her. She was sleeping in bed when a shock appeared to vibrate throughout her body, she shook around in the bed sheets.

My lip quivered and I called out to her "Mom?"

The sound of her coughs echoed around the room, her heavy, frantic breaths screeched all around me.

"Mommy!" I yelled out to her wanting to save her.

In the mirror I watched her attempt to reach underneath her bed for her inhaler, when a soft breeze quivered throughout the room with a deep exhale.

I stood staring at the mirror in a calm silence. Mommy did not get back up into bed.

43 Days After

Dylan

I had to take care of the house for Tamie's return. All the food we had was under the stairs in Mom's bag.

I pulled over my stool so I could have good height over the kitchen counter and pulled out what was left of the food. A tin of peaches, dried apple crisps, and a tin of baked beans. I placed the food into a cupboard all except for the dried apple, which I took upstairs to eat in my room.

"Howdy Sebastian", I greeted my bear as I entered the room. I sat with him for a few hours snaking on the apples together and deciding when we should next go out to find some food.

Finishing the dried apples, I picked up Sebastian and we ran down stairs. I collected my bandana and goggles, tying the bandana around my mouth just as Mom had shown me.

I put on my coat and trainers and was ready to leave.

"Sorry Sebastian but you'll have to stay in the bag", I told him, placing him into Mommy's bag, to protect him from the ash.

I left the house and into the grey clouds of ash, quickly closing the door behind me, not to get the ash into the house. I looked around me, It was like being back in my dreams, the houses around me were barely visible. As I walked along the road, I noticed that our neighbor's house had collapsed. I hoped that my house would not go through the fate, before remembering who had lived there, it was Tamie's friends grandmother. I continued walking down the road to the end of the street wondering if Lily's grandmother was alright and whether she had even been home when the storm struck.

I continued to the end of the street and walked up to a house me and Mom had not yet searched. I looked around the house wondering if I would have to break a window, but fortunately the back door was unlocked. So I stepped inside of the house and into the houses dining room.

I looked around the room, all the lights were off.The walls had a blue tinge through the dark haze, on the walls were family photos, of people I think I saw at last years school fair. I pulled Sebastian out from the bottom of the bag, "Let's find the kitchen, Sebastian".

Sebastian looked around the frame of the door, it was the Kitchen.

We rummaged through the various cupboards

of found dried pasta, rotting fruit (Mom had told me to stay away for that), a tin of biscuits and tinned pineapples, "It a shame that they're not peaches", Sebastian nodded in agreement.

In the last cupboard, I found cake tinnes and decorations, candles and molds and then at the back of the cupboard a bottle of chocolate sauce!

"Look at this!" I pulled out the bright brown bottle to show Sebastian.

After placing the food into the bag, still holding the Chocolate sauce, I put the bag on my back and found a dusty living room. The living room was small but comfortable, they had a cream sofa which took up most of the back wall which I sat down on next to Sebastian. I looked around the room, at the bland art and family portraits.

"Do you think these guys are ok?"

I looked down at Sebastian, took the Chocolate sauce from him and removed the cap.

After trying really hard the lid eventually popped off and flew across the room, me and sebastian laughed as it pinged of a small vase of dry flowers, but the chocolate was worth it. I ate all of it really fast, my tummy hurt a little after and thought I might have a rest on the sofa but decided to get back home, just in case Tamie came back while I was off exploring, So I placed Sebastian back into Mom's bag and went back outside.

the car and approach the boy. The boy shies away walking backwards.

On my way home a car came out of the cloud, and pulled over next to the sidewalk. These were the first people I've seen, and they're strangers. Mommy and Tamie always said don't talk to strangers, so I tried to walk faster.

A man stepped out from the car, and walked toward me while waving. "Hello. Little boy."

"I'm not suppose to talk to strangers." I shouted through my bandana walking faster towards the house. The man smiled and pushed his glasses back up his nose. His smile was warm, though I thought he should have been wearing a scarf like Mom did.

"That's a really good thing, but can you break

that rule just this once." The man crouched down, to talk with me.

"Okay." He seemed nice, so I listened to him.

"Why are you out here by yourself?"

"I'm looking for food."

"Do you want to come with us." The man gestures at the car, where another little boy watched from a window. The boy was much younger than me and sitting on the lap of a girl not too much older than Tamie who smiled kindly to me. "We have food and water. You can have some if you like."

"Tamie will come home with food and water", I declared, "She'll be looking for me".

"Who's Tamie, is she looking after you?"

"She's coming home"

The man looked at me warmly his smile slowly fading to an expression of sympathy.

"It might take Tamie a while to get home fella", he rubbed some ash off from his glasses, "Tell you what why don't you come stay with us for a bit", the man hesitated, "Until she get back".

Tamie wouldn't find me if I went with them.

"No. I don't want to." I took a step away from him.

"Well you can't stay here all alone." he proposed standing up waving his arm through the ash around the empty houses.

"Well how about we just give you a lift home?" The man offered, briefly looking back at the car and then back at me, "Do you know how to get back? We can take you back."

"I can get back by myself. I'm a big boy. I don't want help", and I continued marching back home.

The man sighed behind me. "Okay. I won't force you. Be careful."

The car and drove away and I wondered when Tamie would get back.

Tamie

I was tired and there was nothing for miles. A couple bodies here and there. One of them had a bottle of water, he won't be needing it, so I took it off him. I kicked a rock out of my way. I had seen the odd car in the last few weeks and avoided driving them, they had been driving carefully, through the dust. Now a car came into view that appeared to be driven by a maniac. It came to a halt in front of me.

I saw someone come out of the car, a man, around 6'2, well built with an unattractive, yet distinct, facial tattoo and a knife on his belt. A woman remained in the car, tapping on the dashboard.

"What we got here?" He walks slowly toward me.

I raise the crowbar. "I'm just looking for shelter. Have you seen any nearby? I'm not picky."

"Could come in the car. Rest up real good." He pointed to the car as if I hadn't seen it.

"No a chance."

"Don't take rides from strangers, huh? That's fine. There was a place few miles back-" He pulled his knife and rushed me.

I staggered back, narrowly avoiding a slash at my face. I thrust the crowbar forward, and hit him in the gut with the blunt end. He staggered back, but recovered quickly. Running backward I drop the crowbar, knowing that eventually he would overpower me. He paused until I pulled out the pistol and fired a shot blindly in his direction. I missed, but he stepped back arms raised.

"Easy now, easy now."

A woman who looked like a stereotypical biker chick came rushing out of the car but stopped when I pointed the gun at her.

The woman left the car and walked towards me, almost storming, until I pointed the gun at her.

"Either of you move and I'll kill you. I won't lose sleep over it either."

"I don't believe her." The woman laughed and

took a step forward.

The man motioned for her to stop. "Easy now. I think she will. I think even she wants to. Probably just doesn't want to waste her bullets quite yet."

"Smarter than you look." I smirked a little.

"Little bitch has no respect." The woman scoffs. "We're your elders."

"Could have fooled me."

The man laughs. "I like this chick."

"Thats just cause she looks tight." The woman rolled her eyes.

"Tight or not. We could use a girl like her. Not just for playin with either." The man put away his knife. "How bout you come along with us?"

"What makes you think I'm going to trust you, you attacked me."

"I have a gun. I could have shot you by now. I haven't. You don't need a pulse for me to have fun with ya." The man shrugged.

I eye the car. "Fine. You turn the car around

though. I'm going home."

"That's bull." The woman spat.

The man leant on the hood of the car. "Deal. Can even keep the pistol drawn while we ride. Won't hold it against ya."

We got into the car, the man calmly, the woman and I trying to kill each other with our looks.

"Names Drac by the way." The big man glanced back as me as he started the car. "This here is my old lady, Nanz. Don't mind her, she just gets a bit jealous. What you called?"

"Tamie."

He laughed. "Never thought I'd held at gunpoint by a girl with a name like Tamie. Wouldn't doubt you'd hesitate to gut us if you had to."

"I'm determined."

"I can tell. Well, let me tell ya bout me and Nanz. Get to know each other, that way we won't have to gut each other."

Drac started to talk about their past lives, and past deeds. I catch something about a fire recently, but don't bother paying attention.

44 Days After

Dylan

    I sat at the dining room table, eating from a pack of crackers. My feet swung above the squishy carpet which caught my crumbs, it was like edible ash. Occasionally I would watch the ash floating in the air outside my window. The cloud was lighter, each grey speck slowly drifting to the ground. It had already covered all the flowers.

Sebastian sat on the table watching me draw me with Mommy and Tamie, before the bad weather came. The three of us were sitting on the bench in the garden. I looked up out of the window, but could barely see it. I drew a big sun in the corner of the page with my orange pencil; I had lost my yellow one.

"When do you think Tamie will be back?" I asked Sebastian.

Sebastian didn't know, but it reminded me that it was fortunate that we had recently been shopping as she would probably be back soon. She would know what to do. I nodded agreeing as I reached for another cracker, I held it in my mouth and continued to coloring in the sun.

Swallowing a piece of cracker, I put the orange pencil back into my colours box and reached for a dark bright red pencil, and drew three big smiles onto each of our faces.

"I bet she'll be back soon." I told him.

Tamie

Drac slows the car as we come upon a ranch house.

"Might be able to find something useful in here." as he waved his hand in its direction Drac looked back at me. "Like a maybe a rifle or something."

I shrugged to acknowledge his thinking was probably sound. "It's not exactly out of sight though is it?"

"Watch your tone, when you're speaking to your elders." Nanz's nostrils flared in disgust.

"Hardly relevant anymore. We've all have the same experienced this shit with fresh eyes."

Drac put his hand on Nanz's shoulder. "Watch the car, babe. Tamie and I'll check it out."

I stepped out of the car silently.

Nanz grumbled something about me being a slut, but didn't put up much of a fight.

A couple of moments latter Drac appeared from behind the car with a large hunting knife on his belt and an old looking revolver in his hand.

"Only got one shot. So you're with a pistol if we end up in a shoot out. Unless you don't think you can handle that."

"Better chance I'll suck you off, prick."

"What's the chance of that."

"There isn't."

The front door creaked as Drac opened it to reveal two occupants. I'd have assumed the pair of young men were dead had they not been standing armed with a tiny baseball bat and a two-by-four. The room stank of the infected bandages that adorned their skeletal bodies. Their clothes were just marginally in better shape than they were, although somewhere along the way they had lost their shoes, leaving their feet blackened by ash.

"St.... st.....stay b..... b.....back." The guy

with the two-by-four stuttered as he eyed the pistol in my hand.

"Easy boys." Drac pulled down his mask and placed his hand on the hilt of his knife.

"We're just looking around."

"Nothing's left here. Just some ammo belonging to some gun that's not here." The boy with the bat's voice crackled.

Drac took a step toward the boys, "We could use some ammo. Mind if we take it?" Drac eyed focused on half a bottle of water that lay between the two boys.

"We'll give it to you for some food or water. Fair trade?" Two-by-four nods.

"I think that could be fair." Drac shifted his posture towards me. "What you think darling?"

"Want to see the bullets first, they might not fit our guns." I shifted the pistol to my left hand.

"I think that's fair. How'bout it boys? Show us the ammo, and then we'll decide if it's worth a trade."

The boys slowly nodded. Two-by-Four turned

and opened his bag.

Drac stepped forward purposefully. Knife in hand, before I could react, the room got covered in a fine mist of blood, as Drac slit Two-by Four's throat. Switching the gun back to my right hand and taking aim on the other one.

The air goes deathly silent. Drac swivelled to lock eyes with the boy with the bat.

The boy charged towards Drac, stupidly. He should have run.

Dropping the knife Drac lunged towards him. The boy matched his move dropping the bat. They grappled for a couple of seconds. I started to think that Drac might have met his match, the kid was quick. Spreading my feet evenly I took aim, trying to get a clear shot. They moved with such speed that it was difficult to distinguish where each of their bodies started and stopped. Then remember the knife, I didn't think I just grabbed the knife. I remember being surprised at how easily the knife cut into the boys back. The second time I struck bone, the resistance sent a shock through my body. The boy staggered away from Drac, and crumpled in the corner of the room.

Even before the boy has taken his last breath Drac has started going through their bags. "Fuck! These are rifle rounds! They won't fit either of our guns."

I handed him back his knife, and after he's put it away he motioned for me to hand him over the gun.

"Least they had some food and water."

"Glad this wasn't a complete waste of resources." I rolled my eyes, but doubted the simpleton noticed.

"Let's get outta here."

I shrugged and moved toward the door.

"Did good, darling."

45 Days After

Lily

Having driven for so long, I let my mind wander as I rode my newly found junkyard scooter. The ash blew rough across my exposed skin, but that was the least of my problems. I couldn't see much farther than the very edges of the road.

I remembered my life as it had been before

all of this happened. I missed the quietness of busy university corridor as conversation between friends going from class to class was lost in the static of life. I also missed being able to go outside in a tshirt and feel the sunlight warming my arms. I missed showers and being clean. I tried to imagine exactly what I looked like driving down this desolate stretch of road and I couldn't. I must have looked like some sort of savage. What had I become?

I used to be so strong and confident, but now I was just scared and weak. I was nothing like the person who had started this journey. I wasn't even sure if I could even identify myself in a line up anymore. What did it mean to be Lily? Had I been lying to myself the whole time, thinking that I could go through such a journey and remain the same. Tiredness was starting to take grip, and my eyes had grown heavy.

Having reached the outskirts of town I began to think about my life since I'd left for university. There had been lots that I had achieved whilst away, but at that point as I slowly glided along vaguely familiar streets, it all felt so pointless.

My mind was jolted back to reality as I started to recognised the remains of store fronts from my childhood summer spent with my grandma. I guess this was as good as any place to call home as any of the others that I'd lived in over my life. As I neared the end of my journey my brain kicked up a gear. I thought of all those I'd lost along the way, and as I rounded the corner at the other end of my grandma's street, I started to panic; worried about what I might find when I got home. It was all I could do to keep the throttle pressed.

It was not so far down the the road to my Grandma's house, but in those last few miles my memories dragged me back, further than univeristy, to my parents death. I wanted more than anything to just screw my eyes tight and open them to a sun daubed summer street scene, where I imagine my parents stood with Tamie's parents, whilst my Grandma moved back and forth between here house with big bowls of salad. I didn't wish for a welcome home party, I just wanted a family moment. One that, in old age, I would look back upon in rose tinted fondness.

Gliding down the street, the scooter's engine struggling against the ash clogging the motor, I counted the houses back from the upcoming corner, back to the third one; one, two, and then just space.

What had been Grandma's house was now just an ash covered pile of rubble. I got off the scooter and walked without thinking to stand in the middle of what had been my living room. Grandma was gone. How and where was at that moment completely beyond me, but it was clear that she could not have stayed around here.

At that moment the feeling of loneliness in the bottom of my stomach reemerged with forcefulling. All I had had left in the world was gone.

My knees buckled under my weight. Again my cheeks started to burn as tears forged paths over my ash covered cheeks. Dust pooled around me as I weeped for everything that had been lost.

46 Days After

Lily

    I found myself stood in front of the gap that used to be my house. All that is left now is ruins. My feet are cemented in place as my shock-addled brain thinks of the many of my memories that used to be contained in its walls. This had been my home ever since my parents had perished in that car accident, an event which seemed even further away from my present situation.

I was alone, the remains of a life strew amongst the rubble. Tears ran down my cheeks, scorching like never before. All I had left, at the end of this horrible journey was a feeling of absolute loneliness.

At one point, she hears the voice of a child: "Lily, look what I found?" Dylan is handing her Lily's mother brooch, a lily brooch he found is the debris.

I'm not sure how long Tamie's brother had been stood behind me. But as the realisation of his presence dawned on me my knees almost buckled with gratitude.

"You're alive?", I sobbed reaching out my arms as if I expected him to be just another in a long line of mirages.

I ran forward and embraced Dylan, "I'm so happy to see you here!", I sobbed. "Where is your mother, Dylan?", almost as an afterthought "Do you have any news from Tamie?".

Tears welled at the corner of Dylan's ash-encrusted eyes. He grabbed my arm hoarsely whispered, "Come with me. You need to see Mommy."

Dylan took my hand and insisted that I come upstairs to his mother's bedroom. He told me that she had died, I assumed that this must be the first time he had told someone of his mother's fate, as he was weeping heavily. I had known that she had suffered from asthma so I should have guessed that the ash cloud affected the state of her health.

Even before he lead me up the stairs I could feel the ripe smell of rotting flesh, as it caught the back of my throat.

We stood outside of his mother's door and con- templated who would open it. Dylan stood aside directing me, he was unable to step any further. I was most reluctant in opening the door, but making him do so would have been cruel, so I placed my hand upon the brass handle and entered the room.

The stench hit me, the rotting of the body was severe, and I hesitated as to predict how long she had been dead for. I walked deeper into the room and gazed upon the rotting body.

I keeled as vomit forced its way up from inside my body on to the dusty carpet. It took me a few seconds to settle my stomach, after which I moved further into the room.

I pulled the bed sheets over what remained of her body, and decided that we should bury her body, to put Dylan at some ease.

I grasped the bed sheets around her head, "Dylan, I think we should put your mother to rest, let's take her down to the garden". Dylan looked down at his feet pondering the suggestion. Slowly he looked up to face me and nodded.

Dylan walked into the room and held the bed sheets at his mother feet. "Right, on my mark we'll lift her". Dylan nodded silently. I quickly wiped a tear that was forming to the side of my eye and then I gave the order, "Lift!".

Her body was far lighter than I would have thought, much of her weight must have soaked into the mattress as her body decomposed in the warm stuff room. I walked down the stairs first and opened all the doors. We were fortunate that the ash cloud has dissipated for a brief moment. I thought to myself, "Perhaps, in its own way, even the ash cloud respects the mourning of loved ones."

Entering the garden there is no sign of what was once lush grass which I remember, it was now all carpeted by a thick layer of ash, as was everything else, from the shed to the bushes and the bench. Propped up against the bench was a shovel.

"Dylan let's lie her down here".

We placed the body down into the ash. I went over to the bench and picked up the shovel, I shook off the ash and began to dig a grave. It took me just over an hour before I had a reasonable sized hole. It was by no means traditional, but it would serve its purpose. Dylan tried to help by using a small trowel, whilst his intentions were good, his actual actions helped very little in the overall grave digging effort.

"Okay Dylan, we're going to lay Mommy to rest now", he replied a soft, "OK" exhausted by this afternoons efforts.

We lifted the body and placed it into the grave. We both said goodbye to his mother and I gave a short speech recollecting her kindness which brought Dylan to tears.

After calming him; he returned to the house and I covered the body with the recently exhumed soil.

48 Days After

Tamie

   We walked slowly, the town I had wandered around more times than I can remember completely unfamiliar. Most of the street signs had been knocked over or faded, making the ruined roads difficult to navigate.

   "You're getting us lost, Tamie?" Drac sneered.

"Women don't have a good senses of directions after all."

Nanz snorts. "We even in the right fucking town?"

"Shut up." I glared at the pair. "We're in the right fucking town, but last time I was here it was in one piece with street signs. Now it's gone to shit. So give me a sec." I walked briskly forward, not caring whether the prick and hag followed. I stopped by a mostly intact street sign. Looking back at the other two I say "My house is the next street up.". "Next time, keep your opinions to yourself."

Nanz shrugged whilst Drac chuckled to himself, but nevertheless they followed quietly.

I smiled when we stepped onto my street. The houses were tattered and some had some minor damage to their roofs. My house, was completely filthy, but still in one piece. My eyes fell on rubble that was Lily's house, which has completely collapsed. The thought of Lily's mangled body flashed briefly before my eyes.

I can't help breaking into a jog. "Dylan! Are you here? Dylan?"

As I draw near to the house I saw a boy with filthy hair step out the front door, I can still see blonde through the dust and ash. "Tamie!" Dylan shrill little voice penetrated the grimy air. He sprinted forward to greet me.

As soon as we reached each other I dropped my crowbar and wrapped my arms tightly around him. I can feel tears running down my cheeks. "I was so worried." I pulled down my mask and kissed his forehead and cheeks, while he buried his face into my shoulder. I followed his example and buried my face into his filthy hair, and can't help but smile.

"Tamie?" I looked up to see Lily jogging towards us.

"Oh my God. Lily, you're okay." I smiled at my friend before remembering to pull my mask back up. I unconsciously loosened my grip on Dylan and pulled up his mask to.

When Lily drew near we embraced for what

seemed like an eternity.

"I was worried you were dead."

I kneeled down and pulled Dylan onto my knee. "I can say the same about you." I felt Dylan take hold of my hair, and I took hold of his hand. I noticed the burn on Lily's arm. "Your arm okay?"

Tears brimming in her eyes it was all Lily could do to nod. "Fine. Don't worry."

"I missed you, Tamie." Dylan said as he tugged lightly at my hair.

"I missed you to, Sweetie. I've walked almost all the way here just to see you." I nuzzled the top of his head.

"I was scared you wouldn't ever come back."

"I was scared that you wouldn't be here when I got back." I pull him closer.

My eyes fell on how baggy Dylan's clothes had become. "You've lost a lot of weight, Sweetie."

Dylan leaned against me. "I haven't had lots to eat."

"Well I have a gift for you then." I took Dylan off my knee and removed a can of peaches from my bag. "I kept these just for you." I pulled the can's tab and opened it halfway. "Here."

Dylan's face lit up. "Thank you, Tamie!" He greedily drank the peach juice before he began on the fruit.

I moved closer to Lily. "Where's my Mom? Is she okay?"

Lily shook her head. "She was dead when I got here." She looked at Dylan. "He's been alone for a while now. I don't know how long, but your mom was in a bad shape. I helped him bury her."

I sigh, feeling my heart slow. "I'm not really surprised. Was just kind of hoping, you know?"

Lily hugged me. "I'm sorry."

"Your Grandma?"

Lily shook her head.

"Sorry."

"I'm sure everyone has lost someone."

I glanced over to see Dylan waving toward Drac and Nanz, who stood a little ways back. Lily looked at the pair peculiarly.

"Dylan. So you've been living all be yourself."

I quickly lifted him up.

"Mom got sick, and I took care of her. Then she- she went to sleep and didn't wake up. Then she started to smell. I had to take care of myself. I found food, and made dinner, and made sure I was home as much as I could. In case you came back."

I gave him a quick peck. "You did a good job. It wasn't your fault Mom went to sleep. You were a big boy, and you did the right thing by helping Mom." I held him close.

It was then that I realised that Lily was still staring at Drac.

"What happened on your walk?" Dylan took hold of my hair.

"My walk?" I met his eyes.

He nodded.

"Not a lot. Mostly just walking, walking and searching for food." The smell of fake strawberries came to my mind. "It was really boring." My smile faded.

"When did you meet them?" Lily gestured at

the couple.

"A few days ago." I shrugged. "They helped me get the rest of the way here."

Lily looked at the blood stains on my shirt.

I shook my head, hoped Lily understood.

"I'm not taking care of her fucking brat, or having another slut tagging alone, " Nanz hissed.

"Keep your God damn voice down woman!" Drac snapped back.

I gently put Dylan down and picked up my crowbar. "Stay with Lily, Sweetie."

"I know him. He set fire to the Millers' house!" Lily pointed directly at Drac. "He's the reason their children are dead. They burned to death in that fire."

"Don't go condemning us with the company you keep." Drac gestured at me. "Ain't just the girls hair that's full of fire. I'd swear the bitch came right out of Lucifer's balls."

Dylan

I watched Tamie and Lily talk with the angry
people, one of the dirt covered men brought out a
knife and directed it towards Lily.

"Leave them alone!" I cried attempting to
scare him away.

"Dylan, be quiet now", Tamie insisted moving
me behind her where she knew I would be safest.

"Tamie?" Lily stepped back from the knife
questioning who the people were and if she might
have some help from Tamie.

"Whats the matter Tamie you done with bar-
bequing building?" Asked the man with the knife.

"Leave it Drac", commanded Tamie with an
outstretched arm. I wondered what his name stood
for or if it was in fact his name when I nearly
tripped backwards shocked as Drac stepped closer
still to Lily.

Tamie told me to hide, so I ran to the corner

and peeked my head around to watch. She looked at me hiding behind the corner. But suddenly a crazed woman pulled out another knife and attempted to attack Lily.

"Nanz!" Tamie yelled as she jumped in front of Lily. She took Nanz by the arm and forced the knife out from her hand. She had always beaten me at arm wrestling, and it looked as if she retained her form. With Tamie holding down Nanz Lily was able to hit her across the head with a rock that she found poking up through the ash.

Lily ran over to me, in panic, she wrapped her arms around me, "come on keep your head down", Drac had watched Lily run towards me, but Lily pulled me behind the corner when the gunshot went off. Lily whimpered, as did I, both of us confused and worried as to what was going on.

Four more gunshots rang off. Me and Lily hesitated around the corner to find Drac on the ashy floor. The grey ash slowly turned a murky brown. Tamie's face was blank, expressionless.

Looking into her eyes I was a little bit frightened of the insanity that gripped them so tightly.

I began to cry not this was not my Tamie. Lily pulled me back around the corner and said that we should go back around into the garden of the house, "Where's the real Tamie?" I murmured, Lily took my hand, "That's is our Tamie, Dylan, she's not trying to scare you, she's saving us".

We ran into the garden and past Mum's grave. "Those are very bad men", Lily knelt down to face me, "Tamie is a good person".

From behind the house I heard a woman's piercing scream. I could hear Nanz struggling with Tamie, they were both calling out in a struggle. Lily pulled me to her chest and looked down at me with concerned expression, "I'm sure she's going to be fine" she reassured me. I looked down at my shoes, hoping desperately that Tamie would be okay.

Me and Lily stood in silent in our embrace. It was quiet, and the ash started to slowly swirl around as it started to descend from the grey heavens. I looked up at Lily as she took a deep breath, "Let's go and see if Tamie's all right".

Lily took my hand again and we walked around to find Tamie holding a knife over the body of Nanz.

The ash had started turning the same murky brown colour as Drac. Nanz quivered, shaking and covered in blood, she started to crawl towards us. Lily and me. She gasped for help.

Lily

Nanz was crawling towards me and Dylan. "Help, " her voice quivered and shook in distress, blood gushing from her mouth. I held Dylan's hand tightly and backed away from the half-dead woman crawling towards us.

Tamie slowly walked up behind Nanz throwing the knife down and choosing the crowbar. I gasped in horror at the stranger who walked towards me. Tamie's glazed eyes, full of hatred and murderous intent.

Tamie positioned herself over Nanz her feet either side of her body; and with one swift blow she brought down the crowbar down on the back of her head.

I tried to move Dylan behind me to shield him from his sister's actions, but the crack of Nanz skull reverberates around the street. My attempts in the end were in vain as his head peers around my leg. He sees as much as I do. Perhaps he was right about his sister after all?

"You bitch!" Tamie yell echoed around what remained of the neighbourhood, as she raised and lowered the crow bar for a second and then a third blow.

Exhausted, Tamie dropped the blood-stained crowbar to the ground, spit on the body, and looked up to us.

"That wasn't necessary!"

"What? Not necessary, what do you mean not necessary?" Tamie stepped over the body towards me and Dylan, I moved us both back and Tamie stopped in her tracks, frowning.

"She was defenceless, half dead! There was no need in killing her." I protested and held Dylan back from Tamie.

"She tried to kill us! Not to mention all the other sins I've seen her commit!"

"And what about your sins Tamie?" I stepped forward looking over the corpses, already being claimed by a fresh level of ash.

"Who hasn't sinned, who hasn't had to twist the rules to survive out here!" Tamie's lip quivered as she shouted. She knew the wrong she had done but couldn't face it, or she didn't care.

"These people are dead!"

Dylan ran behind the house and back into the garden in tears. His cries broke the the argument, we both looked at the side of the building where Dylan had run to, both of us unsure as to where to go and what to do.

"Go." Tamie gestured to where Dylan had ran and then turned around to rummage through the pockets of the dead assailants. I sighed, she should be the one going after her brother, and had I not confronted her, she probably would have.

I sat with Dylan on the bench in the garden. We sat in silence, both of us contemplating what we had just seen Tamie do. Tamie had a point, they did try to kill us and had they killed Tamie, Dylan and I would also have been killed; maybe I was the one who was out of touch?

Dylan was the first of us to move. "I'm going inside, " he announced getting up off from the bench.

I looked up at the falling ash and saw the clouds darkening.

"Let's all go back in the house."

Me and Dylan walked back around to Tamie, who was still rummaging through the pockets of her victims. "Shall we go inside?" I looked at Tamie's blood coated face, holding Dylan's hand in a tight grip.

She looked down towards Dylan, and stood up from the corpse. She pulled out a rag from her jean pocket and smiled towards Dylan.

I loosened my grip.

"Sure", she replied. "Let's get something to eat, I'm starving."

She turned to see me sharing her smile; and we all walked into the house.

49 Days After

Sat at a dust covered table, two women and a young boy tuck into a packet of cookies and a bottle of water. The house, as well as the people inside, had certainly seen better days. Just like the world outside there was a dense layer of grey ash covering the floor, piled in corners, and smeared across all their tired faces.

Although they were clearly not in a state to play, one woman handed the boy a box of crayons and a stack of paper. As the makeshift family finished up their cookies and water, the he began to draw again. Once one of the women cleared the table of trash the boy spread his colorful drawings out until they covered the grey, dirty table with colour.

As the women watch the boy scribble away at the paper, one of them sighs deeply, and coughs a bit of ash catches the back of her throat. "I can't believe we're here, " she said solemnly.

"I can't believe we made it, " agreed the other woman.

Looking up at each other the first woman says in a barely audible whisper, "How did it come to this?"

"That doesn't matter anymore, " cut off the second woman, "What matters is that we're together, and we will stay together, no matter what it takes."

"I like staying together, " the boy chimed in happily. The women hadn't even noticed he was listening. Without even looking up he continued with his colouring.

One of the women leaned over to the boy and put a hand gently on his arm. "What are you drawing, " she asked him.

The outside world was harsh and unforgiving now, but inside this house the mood was warm. Through the ashes, the house could barely be seen. It wasn't exactly a fairytale cottage, but the world had moved far beyond that over the past month. The important thing was they would be alright.

THE END

43464379R00229

Made in the USA
Charleston, SC
28 June 2015